'Written in a playful style, ... ploration of the fears and anxieties ... suburban life that seems particularly pertinent as ... from these troubling times' *Big Issue*

'Readers with a taste for unreliable narrators will find themselves entranced by this exhilaratingly peculiar debut. O'Connor's addled language, which often deploys words in ways that don't feel quite right, adds to the delirious impression of a man untethered from reality. Quite where that leaves the reader is all part of the fun' *Daily Mail*

'*Nothing*'s dark and unnerving feel is alleviated by the humour and liberties of the English language at play: bringing to mind Flann O'Brien or Charlie Kaufman, you find yourself at the mercy of your craving for the next page . . . O'Connor's debut novel has already knocked the ball out of the park, and it'll be interesting to see what his next output will look like' *Buzz*

Nothing

Daniel O'Connor

First published in Great Britain in 2021 by Weidenfeld & Nicolson
This paperback edition first published in Great Britain in 2022
by Weidenfeld & Nicolson
an imprint of The Orion Publishing Group Ltd
Carmelite House, 50 Victoria Embankment
London EC4Y 0DZ

An Hachette UK Company

1 3 5 7 9 10 8 6 4 2

Copyright © Daniel O'Connor 2021

The moral right of Daniel O'Connor to be identified as the author of this work has been asserted in accordance with the Copyright, Designs and Patents Act of 1988.

All rights reserved. No part of this publication may be reproduced, stored in a retrieval system, or transmitted in any form or by any means, electronic, mechanical, photocopying, recording, or otherwise, without the prior permission of both the copyright owner and the above publisher of this book.

All the characters in this book are fictitious, and any resemblance to actual persons, living or dead, is purely coincidental.

A CIP catalogue record for this book is available from the British Library.

ISBN (Mass Market Paperback) 978 1 4746 1532 7
ISBN (eBook) 978 1 4746 1533 4
ISBN (Audio) 978 1 4746 1544 0

Typeset by Input Data Services Ltd, Somerset
Printed in Great Britain by Clays Ltd, Elcograf S.p.A.

www.weidenfeldandnicolson.co.uk
www.orionbooks.co.uk

For Em.

WEST SUSSEX LIBRARY SERVICE	
202121983	
Askews & Holts	03-Mar-2022
AF AF	

Nothing?

Against our nothing's reach all things revolt.
As Winter dark will fester darker fears,
A dose of sun has set our shadows dreaming.

Cardenio

28

For six weeks Michael had no shadow, hiding from the white hospital light.

He can still hear you, the nurse would say.

To Esme and the kids, it must have felt as if they were talking down a well.

Daddy's in a very, very deep sleep, she said.

At first the kids needed coaxing to sit by his side. They couldn't get their heads around that thing lying there. But she made it into a game: Daddy was asleep and they were trying to make him dream about their day. Louis, tell Daddy what you did at school. Mara, tell Daddy what you did at nursery. Louis' reading was finally coming on, but he still got stuck on certain words, like 'pail' and 'tumbling'. Mara could imagine a coin falling down a well and never stopping, not even when it reached the bottom. And in the evening Esme lifted her heavy head and went sloshing down the corridor to the toilet, where sometimes she would pee instead of cry.

She leaned over the edge of his bed. Louis had exhausted all of the colouring books in the hospital shop and was drawing pictures of polar bears for a school project, filling them in with white pencil on the white paper. *Isn't he a good little boy*, the nurses said, *staying so well inside the lines?*

Mara always hid behind the chair, giggling while Louis counted.

Ready or not, here I come!

Sometimes he bored of finding her behind the chair and played his computer games while she hid, crashing her toy cars into each other, until Auntie Alex found the pair of them.

Which of my favourite people want cake and bathtime? she asked.

Me, said Esme.

At first, she'd insisted on being the one to wash her husband. Once, she came back from the shop to find that a nurse was halfway through and she asked him who the hell he thought he was.

The next time, she made sure she wasn't around and tried to smile apologetically whenever she saw one of the nurses. The hospital was already responsible for his insides; she conceded to them his skin.

Initially it was immaculate, the way the electric doors slid shut against the diseased world. Then Esme began to notice frayed edges on the curtains, wheelchair frames taped together, toilet lights that flickered briefly. Every other day they would change the sheets. They were bridesmaids to Sleeping Beauty, all white and folding and delicacy. Sometimes she'd watch because it made her husband seem precious. Sometimes she'd leave because it seemed like preparations for a funeral.

*

What do you think he's dreaming of? his mum would ask.

I'll bet it's you, *her* mum would say to Esme, rubbing her shoulders and kissing her cheek. Michael's mum looked disappointed. Esme's mum, who'd come all the way from the other end of the country, wondered aloud if there was anything on telly.

Esme liked to think of him as basking, as if he would wake up livelier than ever. But being so still is enervating. There are marathons of exhaustion that come with quietly fearing the worst.

She kept having this dream (was it a memory? the lines blur with time) where she was supposed to meet him in the pub; there was a match on, and you had to squirm through sweaty bodies to the bar. It had been half an hour now, and he was nowhere to be seen. She kept messaging him. Not upstairs, not down here, nowhere. This place – so thick with people – felt utterly, nauseously empty. She'd wake up panicking. Relieved to find him here, in his hospital bed.

A lot of the time, the machines would be her only company. But there were also occasional nurses, doctors. His parents would come for a few hours. Her sister. Evenings, some friends. Lucas, who came to read aloud the books he'd always pestered Michael to read. The call-centre voices of the mortgage department, who also sounded trapped. But most of her day was spent in the chair beside his bed, fearing. She moisturised his hands obsessively.

Held them, saying, *It's later than you think* – to herself, to the room. But not to him.

In the hours away from work and weather, from outside's shifts and mutabilities, with only the measured, stabilised body of her husband for company, the past ate patches into her days. It was probably the longest she had thought about herself since she was a teenager – those interminable summers of clothes and music and boys and tanning and keeping a diary and sometimes getting so drunk she'd fold into bed on forty hands and feet and wake up furry, caterpillared. All those fantasies that fluttered into her bedroom curtains, into her pillows, of boyfriends, of boyfriends that needed whole oceans of care, of boyfriends in comas. She would have been so jealous of herself.

His mum started wearing a crucifix again, not that she believed in it. Sometimes Esme would catch her murmuring at his bedside, as though she was praying. His mum was proud of herself for more or less holding it all in around Esme.

Oh Michael, she mumbled, rubbing his hand. Not again.

As though he'd made a bad habit of comas. But you can't control what the dead inhabit, or how, so Esme asked if she wanted anything from the shop by the entrance – she was going to see if they had a copy of *Gardeners' World* or, fuck it, *Take a Break*, because there's only so long you can read novels about the coasts of marital strife alongside the sad tide of your comatose husband.

But sometimes she could be practical, too, his mum.

Well, she said, at least they won't sack him now.

? said Esme.

It doesn't look good, does it, sacking someone when they can't even hear you?

Redundant, said his dad, touching her hand.

Exactly.

The sandwiches generally tasted of mulch, but her apple was nice and shiny – only a small dent on the surface. But when she bit into it, the bruise was deep and manky. Seeing her crying, Louis came over with his open bag.

Do you want a crisp, Mummy?

She let it melt in her mouth, trying to not cry any more.

Daddy's counted a gazillion sheep! Mara announced whenever a new doctor or nurse entered. It was part of Auntie Alex's attempt at explaining things, *Your daddy's just counting sheep, their woollen tails and woollen bellies.* The kids were allowed to stay there with Mummy on weekends, but most school nights Alex would take them home for bathtime and stories and a game of Daddysleeps, where they would be as still as possible for as long as they could and the first one to move lost and had to be a dog or a horse or a rat, and even though Alex thought it was a bit morbid she didn't know how to stop it.

One night, Esme *completely fucking lost it* and deleted everything on her phone – photos, apps, accounts, anything that so much as mentioned him. Used his thumb to open his phone and did the same. It was exhilarating – a total emptiness, a complete evisceration, the whole lot cut out, gouged clear, down to the simplicity of a white room. Of her. Of him.

As she caught up with a detective show she'd missed because she was crying in the toilet, she took a new picture of him between bites of her Twix. Deleted it. Took it again.

He lay there, the bastard, without a care in the world.

Esme tried hating the chairs, the plastic curtains, the spit-floating-in-a-swimming-pool effect of the floor tiles. But chairs and curtains and tiles don't hurt. She hated the nurses, hated the doctors. Her spite was smothered by care, by patience. So she tried hating him. He was a bastard, after all, leaving her to cope with two kids and a husband in a coma. This was fun. She could sit there saying, *Wake up, dickhead! What, are you just gonna lie there all day, you lazy little shit? I'm leaving you for a doctor or, fuck it, the next man that stands up, you horizontal twat!* She'd say it quietly enough that nobody on the corridor heard, but loud enough to feel it. She could hope his balls turned to granite. That his United would stay trapped in lower-league promotion battles. Or even better, that he'd wake up and be absolutely fine, except for something innocuously embarrassing – a lazy eye; mispronouncing things; that he'd forget how to tie his laces. He'd catch her laughing. She desperately wanted to tell him the curse she'd put on him, that he'd never be able to find shoes that fit, and he'd go around forever wincing on his corns and everyone would think he had piles. And – she tried this – squeezing his hand, shaking his arm a little, saying to him, *I've given you corns, you prick* – saying it right in his ear, because what if he laughed? What if he just sat up and laughed?

★

Once, just once, Michael's dad sighed aloud, thinking of his own dad. The dead go off like a grenade and leave behind a deafness that rings out in the ears. But his dad had *come back from the war*, and if you ever pulled the pin out of his Sunday afternoon naps, the whole house came down.

I hate watching people sleep, he said.

His mum rolled her eyes, as if to say, *He'll complain about anything.*

His dad shivered,

That's someone walking over your grave, that is, said his mum.

then sloped to the shop, after looking at his son as though the button was broken and you couldn't change the channel.

At night, the place was lit up in blue-dark lights like an aquarium, and walking past the wards for a chocolate bar or *a turn* you could feel the heaviness of all those bodies, floating there. Esme worried about blackouts. Failed generators. Kept on at Alex, whenever she offered to bring clean things, to bring candles.

Esme was no longer wearing her best pyjamas. Lucas stopped bringing things to read to him.

He'd shout through the house, said Michael's mum, *I'm going to Luc's*, and then he'd come back all covered in muck.

Luc didn't know if he was supposed to apologise. He tried reminding Michael of when they were boys – jumping the ditch (Michael didn't make it); constructing a time machine out of a cardboard box and a potato clock (neither of them made it); of all the times Michael had had enough of him and locked himself in the bathroom while Luc sat against the door in his friend's house, trying to coax him out. When Esme closed her eyes, their voices sounded almost the same. After a few weeks, he just came to stare and talk to her. They sat next to each other, either side of Michael.

Just like old times, he said.

She laughed.

She imagined him in bed.

Mara sat on his knee and Esme bit her lip, blinked, weightily. He always brought her coffee, played with the kids.

What are you going to do? he asked once, heavily.

She half-smiled at him, as if he might already know, or almost know. He felt guilty for asking.

Sometimes, with everyone gone, she'd climb up on to the bed and lie beside him, her old earphones strung between them listening to the songs they listened to when young and learning to lean quietly against each other on coaches, on trains, in a lovely slowness against the pacing world, the split music meeting in their heads.

But lying there – all those wires – like that was uncomfortable; she couldn't take it for long.

Over the top of the magazine (she bought it, even though it had a disappointing picture of a black hole on the front, because it felt real, or more real than the news on her phone) it looked a bit like a mannequin – him. You could almost mistake it for the man who tried to take her for a romantic walk along the beach, the man she soaked, kicking up the sea at him (God, she felt like such a knob). The man who arranged a classical fancy dress party for her birthday (because he knew she loved ancient things and fancy dress), fashioned her as Helen, and instead of coming as Paris or Achilles or Hector made himself into a giant horse, got stuck in the bathroom, and had to be freed by two legionnaires and the Minotaur. The man who rubbed her back and kissed her neck and was nearly here, in bed: he almost looked real.

But – she'd been thinking about emailing work about the Vedas exhibition, budget stuff, and she'd have to see if they had anything she could get Lia from work for her birthday in the garage over the road from the hospital (*Vogue*? Red Bull? a warning triangle and hi-vis vest?) – it caught her, for a second: looking at this thing under the blanket, with its eerie gasps, its wires, its bagged liquids, her husband's lifeless face: *What if it woke up?*

27

It come out of nowhere, said the woman who found him.

The local newspaper corrected it to 'came'. No one could find the guilty ball – *It must've ran down the drain or something* – so if she hadn't witnessed the whole thing (she hadn't), the police might never have put two and two together.

It weren't like no one shouted *Fore!* or nothing, she added.

LOCAL MAN IN GOLF BALL COMA – Alex came into the hospital holding the paper, laughing.

What's a 'golf ball coma'? D'you reckon if we hit him with a 9-iron it might wake him up?

While Alex read the article aloud: *Father of two, Michael, was reported to have been walking by the edge of the golf course when a ball strayed over the boundary and collided with his head.* Her sister imagined herself lashing his temple with a golf club. It wasn't the worst thing she had imagined. *His wife, Emse –*

Emse!!

– *Emse was left in a state of 'utter bewilderment' at his bedside in intensive care.* Did she say that? She didn't feel utterly bewildered – if anything, she felt unbewildered, as though the forest had been razed around her and all she could see now was horizon everywhere. The words they'd found felt as far away from reality as that body beneath the bedsheet felt from Michael. But they made it – if not true – real.

The report said he was stabilised, delivered into the ambulance. You'd suppose the traffic unzipped for his flashing lights. Police, meanwhile, beetled around the patch by the golf course, taking measurements and pointing to things. No one owned up. When they made cursory inquiries at the golf club, it transpired that nobody was playing on the range when he was hit. (It was agreed, though, that compensation would be paid and the netting would be extended.)

Not that she thought it was entirely his fault, but none of this would have happened if Michael and Esme hadn't fled the city for a commuter-belt estate a decade or so old, coiled like a shell on the snail-paced village in which he grew up.

It's the kind of place the government wants you to live, said their friends in the city when Michael and Esme announced their intention to move back home (*his* home, at least). But their childless minds were already made up. Esme was concerned that the humid air of their flat above the laundrette would make for damp, soapy kids; Michael was scared of city youths. Finally, she'd had enough when he was mugged on his way back from the takeaway by a man wielding acid. All he took was Michael's wallet, phone, mixed vegetables in a black bean sauce, kung po lamb, two egg fried rice and a large sweet and sour sauce, prawn crackers and chopsticks he had no intention of using – but it was enough. The buildings edged in a little closer. More of the city was shadow. She was having nightmares about taking an elbow to the womb or being pushed in front of a train. Michael walked home with his door keys in blades through his fist. And even though he agreed that it was exploitational labour, delivery men brought their Friday-night dinner.

What's the use? Esme despaired while they sat waiting nervously for the pizza's buzz at their door. You can't punch overcrowding, or air pollution, or house prices.

The commuter belt brought them two children – one before the other – so that by the time the second came around they were almost fully weaned from themselves. Everything became terrifying: stairs, drawers, cupboards, tables, coughs, no coughs, family histories. *Children are a journey*, the book said, a journey in which their genes were planted like roadside bombs. They couldn't watch nature documentaries without feeling inadequate or culpable. Hid their sharp edges as best they could and were cornered by the fear of small, soft heads charging into things. Stairs winced footsteps. The cupboard had begun to hoard smells. When they tickled the kids, their giggles flitted into the fabrics like moths. Glancing, now and then, at their own faces hung on the walls, it was almost impossible to imagine what they would make of the people they were looking out at. Was this the house they wanted to live in? Were these the children they anticipated? *Shut up*, they said to their younger, wide-awake selves, *we're happy*. Fattening with worry about Mara and Louis, while the thin minds behind the faces on the walls quietly feared they'd never have kids at all.

They spent so long worrying about not having kids, it was only right before Louis was born that Esme worried about actually having one. She annoyed herself, fretting that her husband would neglect her for their bab. Though she sometimes found it hard to let herself go like he did, she'd smile through the kitchen window while their dad ran around the garden after the kids, drenching each other in laughter. The dad who was capable of hunching the full twelve foot of him through the smallest door of their imagination, inhabiting their kingdom of snail shells, broken branches, the slim abyss behind the shed. Who at bedtime reminded her of an orangutan, scooping up their sleepy children and helping them to clamber over the drops in the world across his ridiculous limbs. Sometimes she was amazed they ever got here at all; it was so far for them to fall.

Esme described it to her friends as *leafy*. In the city, you had to share a square metre with two other people, but out here each was occupied by 0.6 people; 0.6 people smiled and said *Hello*. They only carried knives if vegetables or animals were involved. Were only fractionally less interesting than *real* people. Sometimes, in the garden, listening to them over the fences, Esme worried about becoming one, gossiping about house improvements and local dogs; she worried about dwindling – remembered that Michael was only 0.6 of a person until he moved to the city. Lucas's voice played in her mind: why reduce yourself to that nowhere that Michael and I grew up in? That smudge between here and there? That shithead's bardo? Why not do it properly, move to a real wilderness, be self-sufficient, resilient? Where Luc saw absence, they saw just enough room to grow into. The trees on their estate had stopped being saplings, but were still too thin to bear children. When they were planted, the golf course was listed among the *chief attractions* of the houses. The managers of the course erected a wall of conifers along its border with the estate. As far as she knew, nobody on the estate *golfed* (as Michael's mum put it). On the toilet, though, you could watch the parabola of shots over the treetops, projecting the rest. Sometimes missing balls would arrive in their garden. They let the kids keep the money for returning the balls to the course. Louis was saving up to buy football boots. Mara was saving up to buy a ghost. The man in the security hut who collected the balls referred to the kids as 'golden retrievers', and when they eventually worked out what this meant they barked all the way home.

Michael could remember none of this. There was nothing. Except he remembered that he'd stooped (because he was a good citizen) to put his dog's crap (which was biodegradable) into a plastic bag (which was not), making his way along the dirt path beside the golf course when he woke up mid-step in the hospital, flat on his back

26

feeling as though he'd been hit on the head. He was perfectly tucked in and completely stunned. At first, he was only thoughts (*Uh?*). Then a nose, too. He could smell her – she smelled unplaceably familiar and antiseptic.

Where's Max? he thought. No stench of dog. No bag of dog crap. *Max?!*

He could see the sad-eyed dog panting a hot, meaty grief over his comatose face, whining. So vivid, so tangible – it made no sense that he was here in a hospital bed, not walking his dog.

For a couple of days his wife(?) had been flitting over him, looking at herself on the sheen of his corneas. She kept telling him that he was in the hospital, that there'd been an accident, and that she loved him. This was new to him.

She was wearing slippers outside of her house. The place was full of greetings cards; had he missed a birthday? Everyone smiled when they saw him as if he was the punchline to a joke. He was full of questions and completely speechless.

★

A doctor said *subdural haematoma* as though she was introducing herself. They already seemed to know who he was. Prodded and flexed his body with illegible twists of their lips. When it came to his actual state, they gave nothing away. Nothing felt more terrifying than nothing, or more real.

With glottal-thick guilt, he watched the nurses being delicate with bits of his body so far beyond his control that they wouldn't even flinch under a dropped brick. Once, when they washed him, he could feel, or thought he could feel, the damp near him – a wet numbness ghosting somewhere where his arms ought to be; the thought of being sponged on his feet, his legs, and the terror of never stepping foot into water again – which he held, as if the chill memory of the sea could frighten his legs awake. That fear of paralysis he could feel trickling between his toes.

His parents(?) visited for hours at a time. If their faces were a smudge blurry still, their muted disappointment was familiar. His mum said *Oh* repeatedly; his dad put the football on the television and picked the side he wanted to lose, grumbling, guttural. Every time Michael expected a cross-field pass or a shot they seemed to spoon it into the stands.

Football, his dad tutted, as though the game had been reduced to irony.

Something. That tut was something. A percussive touch. And he remembered something of himself: being marched to the match by his dad, the vibrations of the old stand responding to all those feet; him, tall enough to just catch the heads bobbing about on the pitch – eating sweets out of his dad's coat pocket, the steaming piss-trough at half-time; the fag-ash mascot with his head off, trouncing a pie in the concourse; the small bird stuck, clapping in the corrugated roof. And, into adulthood, still sitting beside this man at the match. His dad, tutting. His dad.

He blinked at them, tremulous. His mum cried.

Michael!

Then his dad.

As though he'd come home after being so far away, almost the semblance of the son they'd expected.

Later, Esme(?) saw him twitching his fingertips on the sheets and cried, and cried and laughed, laughing and holding his hand. She didn't seem to notice him looking at the door. And she held him there, crying and laughing, and telling him

You're back – I've got you back.

He didn't know where he'd been. He couldn't remember being anywhere with her. When he imagined getting up and making a run for the door, he saw his legs crumple into their shadow.

If anything, imagining the worst seemed to expedite his recovery. He lay there, waxy as a Catholic saint, with miraculous anxiety. Every visit, the doctors would be amazed by some renaissance in his faculties – a twitching toe, an elbow bend – while he was worrying about his atrophy in a specially adapted, damp downstairs annex. He imagined that a sequence of carers would become his closest human interaction, sponging and spooning him new dependencies. (He could raise an arm!) This Esme would visit him, un-widowed and griefless, with asphyxiating patience and a resentment that expressed itself as love. (He flicked her hand!) His parents would die; and thinking of them, immobilised in their coffins, he'd feel closer to them than he had done for years. (He pointed to the cup of water!) To these kids, the ones hiding behind the chair in the corner drawing pictures, forbidden to ever think bad thoughts about their dad, he'd be nothing more than a strategy for appearing nuanced and interesting to people they wanted to sleep with. (He turned his head!) And there, still, is his wife, remembering how they fed their children as she lifts the spoon to his mouth – humiliations worn dry of any humiliation – wiping the slobber from his chin. (He coughed a vowel!) He'd never be able to tell her that he hated her, that he wished she'd disappear – the most he could ever manage was to strop his mouth like a toddler and grunt

Uhsme?

His voice surprised him.

Uhs-me.

Her hand was over her mouth, trying not to let herself believe that it was true, because it still might not be true. Restraining her shudders from crying through his thin-boned body. Mara sprang up on to the bed and gripped his leg in case he got away. Louis bit his fingers by the window.

Michael!

Michael.

She rubbed away the tears with the nub of her thumb.

Oh God, Michael. Where the hell have you been?

He could manage a nod, indifferently.

Mara, clambering over the bed, had snarled up the covers by his feet. They must have been cold – vague and far away, still not feeling as though they were quite a part of his body – because they'd put socks on him. But he could feel her prodding his face, he could feel her laughter convulsing through him.

Everybody was laughing. Everybody was crying. And as Esme was about to pour on to him she held back, seeing his mouth about to speak. Because for over six weeks she had waited for him to speak, to reassure her that whatever else had happened to him, all of this love hadn't gone to waste – that he was still capable of being loved. His voice was unclear, hallway-hidden in his throat. She leaned in close to hear him tell her he loved her.

My sock, he said, pointing with a weak finger.

She smiled at him, with her hand over her mouth. *My sock* – it would make a cute story, the way Louis' first word was 'elf'.

But he stared at her until she stopped laughing and, delicately, removed his sock, turned it the right way out.

It's all right, said Esme, trying her hardest to hide it.

It's fine, said a doctor, a little memory loss can be expected in the circumstances. We'll monitor it, but the forgetting should ease.

This doctor had his arms folded and kept patting himself reassuringly, twitching his nose kittenishly as he listed issues: mobility, speech, amnesia . . . the whole dark and disorientating return from the cave. *It can also make you a prick*, his smile added. The walls looked aside as though they were sniggering.

Fine, the doctor repeated. Fine.

His waking presence was a non sequitur. Hers a tautology. Only the paraphernalia of this wife's fretting around his bed made his imaginary weeks seem real: the worn bristles of her cheap toothbrush, two pairs of slippers and a pair of trainers with laces so loose they could be declared defacto slippers. Her laptop snoozed in the armchair like a cat. This was her world now, and it wasn't clear she was ready to give it up. Whoever she was, he said to himself, she must really like him to let herself go like that. (The

Michael he'd caught in the mirror – gauzy and shrimped, being helped up by this attractive woman – wasn't so assured.)

They ate sandwiches from a tray over his bed with nothing to talk about. She'd spent the last six weeks sitting at some estranged man's bedside and he'd been asleep. When she spoke, it was as though someone had cut phrases out of a magazine. He gathered from the clippings of her conversation over these few days that she was underpaid for something unfulfilling in a museum, something to do with corporate sponsorship (the diffuse anxiety of credit-card debt struck him from somewhere before the golf ball). Apparently, he worked in insurance – which didn't sound right, so he didn't mention it, in the hope that they forgot and he could work in football or TV.

A stranger had shaved him clumsily and he was wearing someone else's pyjamas. She kept touching her hair, anxious at the grease and the frayed ends; her sandwich couldn't hold itself together. It was the worst first date he had ever been on.

When he sat up a little, she smiled and said,

You've got your shadow back.

And the way he looked at her in reply, she may as well have invited him to join a cult.

There's only a small window during which you can tell your wife that you have no idea who she is before it becomes a touch awkward. He hoped instead that she'd intuit it from the way he'd forgotten who won the last World Cup or how much he despised tinned tuna. *How could he possibly remember me*, he imagined her saying, *if he can't even remember which day's bin day?*

★

How's Max?

It seemed as though she was trying to remember him – then smiled, faintly.

Can he come and visit? I miss his stupid tail.

He kept remembering himself pulling on the dog's lead (he was the only thing Michael could properly recall), as though this could tug something of himself from the dark undergrowth of the coma. He wondered why no one had brought him in yet to aid his recuperation.

I don't think the nurses would take kindly to a dog on their ward.

But people can go to the vet.

She had no answer. He threw his hands up in exasperation.

The place was full of imbeciles. It only took another doctor to step into the room for Michael to roll his eyes.

I was walking the dog, he said before she'd asked.

How many times had they been through this now? Doctors kept striking him with the same questions, as though they were tuning a piano. Whenever he mentioned the dog Esme looked away, sometimes teary, sometimes biting her cheek.

I was walking the dog, he said, and then I woke up here.

And as he answered questions, people glanced at the bandage still (needlessly) sabotaging his head. Even he couldn't rely on himself to be himself. Or *that* self, *their* self, his . . . because he was *a* self, in him, and that made him *him*, didn't it? But he worried they had him – this Esme, these parents – and he had nobody. Or that he only really existed between him and them, the deeper, shaded overlap, this – the darkest stretch of his three shadows from three different lights reaching for the plastic cup of water at his bedside table.

Fuck, he said at Esme, as though it was her fault he'd spilled the water so pathetically over himself – except when he looked, the cup was minding its own business on the bedside table, holding the water he'd expected to be soaking into his sheets. Esme smiled as though she wasn't quite sure who he was, either.

The kids were kids; every so often he'd catch them stealing a bit of his face and wearing it better, which was lovable and unnerving. But if they seemed familiar, it was mostly in the way that all kids do, before their symmetry has had time to drift into adulthood's incongruities. They arrived either sheepish or tearful. They'd only just got used to Sleeping Daddy; now he was awake again but tired, very tired, even though he'd been asleep for weeks. The whole thing felt like a practical joke and he couldn't tell if they were in on it or not.

Hello, he said.

Hello, they said back, mocking his voice.

The boy was in the *did you know* phase. *Did you know that when Mara was in Mummy's tummy she was in seawater and when Mummy cries she cries little drops of sea? Did you know dolphins can hear ultrasounds and salmons can feel magnets? Did you know you weren't asleep?*

The answer is always *No.*

★

It all felt disgustingly unclean, as though he was wearing somebody else's body. The sores on his shoulders, his bum. His first piss after they removed the catheter from his penis; the way it whistled like a seamy uncle leaving the church after a long August funeral.

But, terrified he'd be forever bedridden, Esme-dependent, or worse, he made a *remarkable recovery*. The adults murmured behind his curtain. One of them drew it and announced

You can go home.

Nobody noticed him grip the sheet.

25

That last night, waiting through hospital discharge procedures, felt like the evening before a wedding. All exuberance and terror in the guise of logistics. Plenty of people offered a lift, but Esme decided they'd take a cab home. She was half-right: it sort of made it feel like they'd come from the airport, pulling up outside the front door with their bags and a new skin tone. As estranged, as unhomely. Michael glanced around the estate suspiciously; it wasn't how he'd pictured it. This can't really have been his house, staring at him with the stolid face of a BBC news presenter. Had he lost a bet? Gone through some sort of government re-education programme? The boughs of the tree outside their door nodded and he reached up to a leaf the way you'd touch the face of an unfamiliar horse. Then noticed himself doing it.

What's the matter?

Nothing, he said.

The blonde bob across the road waved (sarcastically?), unloading shopping from the Nissan; he half-smiled back. There were people here. He was part of this.

★

The kids were skittling about: laughing inconsolably and crying infectiously and quietly playing with things on the floor. Alex had bleached the life out of the house for them; the medical smell eased the disorientating transition a little. Still feeling dislodged and weirdly vertical, having intruded on his own body, Michael wore a shirt for the occasion, intending to make a good first impression on his home. The place had an elusive familiarity about it, the way rooms in dreams are almost rooms you know.

Where's Max?

Oh, said Esme. He's at Alex's. She raised her finger as if she'd just had the idea, then tried to hide it by rubbing the back of her head. Alex has been looking after him.

Oh, he said. Oh.

We've got a mouse, she said, as though it was a consolation prize.

She brushed her hair behind her ear, nodded along with herself.

I keep meaning to lay one of those traps, the humane ones – but part of me just wants to bash the furtive prick with a tenderiser.

No!

His affront drained slowly as he realised she wasn't being entirely serious. They stared at each other a moment in misunderstanding, then drifted apart.

Although his face was framed here and there, he wasn't going to take the blame for the decor. He could barely bring himself to sit on the chair, hunched around his tea (from a proper mug!) like somebody who'd just been rescued from the sea.

I'm making your favourite for dinner, said Esme. Don't get used to it.

But when he sat down at the table after hours of glaring at the TV, there was a dish of lasagne fainting.

Are you OK? she said, with her hands still in the oven gloves. Have you got a headache?

Lasagne, he said drily, my favourite.

Louis was already dipping garlic bread into the saucy surface. Mara was carefully investigating each of her peas, deciding whether to exile it to the floor.

Banish him! laughed Mara, dropping a pea.

(*Where did she get that?* said the look on Esme's face. *Some cartoon?*)

Stop it, Mara!

The peas – he knew his temper was fraying, tried to bend the fork with his thumb – the girl throwing the peas; his patience couldn't take the thought of the peas on the floor. Kept picturing their dented bodies, sulking on the wooden boards.

Sorry, she said with an attempt at a smile.

Banish him!

Mara!

Michael huffed, leaning down to gather the peas from the floor, except there were no peas on the floor, just his feet, Esme's feet, the kids' dangling feet. Now he felt like an idiot: the peas had scarpered, God knows where. And when he surfaced from under the table, Mara was smiling at him beautifully.

Careful, Mara, said Louis. Or you'll end up on the naughty step.

Esme looked at him apologetically, as though she'd let

bad habits slip in on her watch – her children playing up. Their children, he had to remind himself. Their children.

The boy kept showing him pictures of melting glaciers, as though now he'd woken up he could do something about it.

Terrible, isn't it? said Michael, sensing that wasn't quite how you speak to children.

Louis kept swiping through, *look at this one . . . look at this one*, with more pictures of rocky mountain tops. It was interminable.

He retreated to the toilet; its locked door. Esme passed him smiling on the stairs; the seat was warm from her bum. Inappropriately familiar; familiarly inappropriate.

A golf ball shooting-starred over the treetops. He wished he was alone, in a flat somewhere, watching crap football.

I need some fresh air, he said.

Hold on, said Esme, trying to hide her anxiety, we'll all come.

But he insisted on going alone, escaping while she was caught between trying to look after him and the kids.

Outside was invigoratingly normal, even if he couldn't walk far. He puzzled his way to the row of shops at the edge of the estate – the usual newsagent & hairdresser & vape shop & dog grooming & misc. takeaway identity parade. None he recognised. Michael was half-thinking of flagging a police car to tell them he'd been kidnapped from hospital and brought here (*Where am I?!*) to this nowhere commuter-belt town, when he glanced up to the windows of the flats above the shops. This evening breathing through their thin glass – the same tired windows, the pigeons squatting on the roof above them. The geography of the place settled on him. Sitting on those bollards, sharing chips with Jenny whom he was going to marry.

Ha! he said, staring at the thing, one hand on his cheek.

The woman jogging by gave him a weird look – this man, amazed at a bollard. Jenny! Why wasn't he married to Jenny? They were going to go travelling (once she'd been to drama school) and then move to California and live in the hills. The man from the vape shop was pulling the shutters down (spray-painted with *Jonny milks bulls*), arse-crack badgering out into the evening air. This wasn't California!

Shuffling back to the house they'd brought him to, half-lost and almost walking into things, he searched for Jenny on his phone. He didn't have her number or anything, but she was easy enough to google. Working in publicity for some production company. Married, by the looks of things. At the sight of her and some man – sunset, champagne, beach – he stopped in the street, looked around: sullen hedges, skulking cars, birdmush in the middle of the road. *What the fuck?* In all of those photos there was no trace of him missing from her smiles. But him and Jenny – bollards and chips! – sex in the park and big plans and they shared fucking chips! How had he not lived his own life?

He shook his head almost the whole way back.

Nice walk? said Esme, pretending not to hurry to the door.

Huh, he said. And meant it.

When it was bathtime, Michael pretended he needed a lie-down after his six weeks of lying down and found his way upstairs. Mara was splashing through the walls, asking why Daddy kept getting Daddy wrong. He stared at the ceiling, the small crack in the paint spreading into a photon ring of yellowish damp; he was still scared of falling asleep.

With the kids tucked up, Esme came in to see how he was getting on, lounging there on the bed. She was chatting at him, idly, as she undressed. At first, she didn't notice the way he was half-glancing at her, unsure if he was allowed – then staring; from the nervousness in his eyes she read a sense of it, that there was an unknownness to the moment. Their faces wore that *Now?* look. Should they at least turn the light off?

But now it was happening – she was taking her clothes off – walking over to his side of the room – as though it could still be innocuous – stopping beside him – close enough – her thigh or his hand might accidentally touch – turning to face him – a breath's width apart, he thought of kissing her and then – nothing.

The approaching moment, whatever it was, had been frightened off. The wardrobe stood awkwardly in the corner, the lamp looked away. He watched the crack spreading across the bedroom wall (*built on the cheap*, he said to himself, trying to think non-sexual thoughts). She stumbled into her comfy joggers.

I'm terrified you know more about me than I do, he didn't say to her.

I'm terrified there's bits of me lost in you forever, she didn't say to him.

So they sat in bed with Esme's laptop playing reruns of programmes Michael had never seen before, the pair of them scrolling elsewhere on their phones – thinking of other people, thinking of each other, neither of them daring to mention that, for better or worse, *we are condemned to one another.*

At some point, she turned the light off.

Feeling like an intruder, he'd balled himself up as tight as possible in bed. It had been creepy enough seeing her underwear drying on the airer, now her warmth was with his warmth under her duvet. Whenever a car passed he could see the photograph on the bedside table: her face and his face, just married. She'd pretty much kept her looks, and Michael was jealous of the *lucky fucker* who resembled the brother he'd never had, kissing her so comfortably. (They'd have to get thicker curtains.) He was an ex – out of Michael's body, but not necessarily hers. The man she'd tended in the coma.

But the diamond ring on her finger in the photograph; he remembered the sickly, oily puddle of waiting to ask – the shearwater, fishing off the rocks in twos and threes, fat stupid fish leaping out from the surface. That was all: not her, not what he said, not anything other than anxiety, the ring, the water on the rocks.

He conceded: that was him in the photo, them – beside themselves, on the bedside table. Whatever the trajectory of that couple stepping out into the blossom (marriage! children! adventure!), it hadn't arrived at him. Or didn't feel as though it had. He felt cut out from himself.

You still awake?

Esme had rolled over. He felt the breath of her voice on the hair of his ears. Even with his body still almost in abeyance, it was something.

Michael—

This was it, he thought: the day he's come home she's going to ask for a divorce. He imagined it was all too much, the strain of his coma. Some wives would kill for an inert husband; not her. He prepared himself to look disappointed, but understanding – appreciative, even, of her coma vigil. Under the circumstances, etc. etc. Presumably he loved her once, but rebuilding that – it seemed too intricate, too hard. He could be cowardly: imagined himself happily alone, playing video games in his pants, watching Portuguese football, eating breadsticks for dinner . . .

Michael, she started again.

She sounded a little confused, derailed. As she touched his arm, he noticed she wasn't wearing her engagement ring. She must have disowned it already.

There's something . . . we need to talk. But. There's something I need to tell you.

Yeah?

While you were in the coma—

What . . .

You know, the dog.

Max?

The room returned him his voice; it sounded lost and fearful echoing from the pastel walls, the wardrobe, the happy photos. She was on the verge of it – he could tell – of saying something terrible. And all that comatose time, when he woke in the hospital it felt as though Max had been beside him the whole way, licking his face, the fog of his breath rolling into his sleep. The dog – or, to be precise, the dog's crap – was his first thought coming to, and near enough the only thing he'd managed to rescue of himself from the coma's underland. Now he'd been home a day and almost forgotten him completely.

He coughed, guiltily.

Yeah, Max, she said, well – he went missing.

She looked confused, as though this wasn't quite what she'd expected herself to say.

What?

We looked for him everywhere, but—

You lost my fucking dog?

Michael sat up – he could see her dim shape pleading in the dark.

He just.

How?

You know what dogs are like. They get carried away. We looked everywhere.

Not Max, though. He wouldn't.

Michael—

He faffed after the light switch. The lamp glowed

hesitantly, as though it didn't want to be dragged into things. Esme was squinting at him.

Did *you* look for him?

Course. We did everything. But . . . We had a lot on. I was looking for you, most days, she said, squeezing his hand.

Did you look in the hospital? Maybe he came to find me.

By now he was standing outside of the bed, head in hands, wanting to say something cutting and final – but since he'd woken from the coma he'd struggled to remember what order words go in. And her look clattered him: a look of love, with all the fear that love brings, its long comet's tail of grief. He could see it meant something, suggested a lineage of destruction and repair, all of their increments and deflections, but he knew basically zero of what brought him to here, in his boxers (atrophied, but with a smudge of flab), stepping out of the dark to the end of her bed.

Michael—

There was little she could say. Taking his forgetfulness out on her, he stormed out of the room triumphantly (he pictured himself departing like a haughty Caesar!) until, a few steps from the door, he crumpled like a newborn calf.

She rushed over,

Michael!

holding his shoulders, sitting him up.

I'm fine, he said, brushing her off. I'm fine.

She was fussing over him.

He glowered at her with the dog in his eyes; it was as though he was looking at her from nowhere.

24

It seemed more dignified to give the dog his full name. The next morning, Esme watched from the window while Michael dug a hole in the garden and planted a log with 'Maximian' and the dog's dates penknifed into it. The kids were cajoled into attending the memorial in the garden where they each said their favourite thing about Max, but he was neither

Floppy and glittery and spacebouncy!

nor

More fiercer than ten tigers and fast as three white leopards

so only his eulogy to Max's earnestness and loyalty counted. Then they ate hot dogs (Louis' suggestion), and Esme folded the picture Mara drew of Max as a purple puppy and stored it in the recycling.

He'd wanted to invite some other people, but he was having trouble recalling who other people were and Esme seemed embarrassed about the whole thing. So he sat there in the garden slurping coffee and staring at the memorial log, thinking of how he'd have to replace it with something more permanent – whatever material they use to store nuclear waste, that kind of permanence. Mara wouldn't go near the log after Louis told her he'd heard it growl. But now she petted it, *Good boy*, while Louis had given up trying to get it to chase a stick and was throwing a toy dog for the stick to chase instead.

The memory of their weight on his shoulders, pointing (*Wow!*) at simple things – had he imagined this? Whenever he saw those dads (making a virtue of their largeness, simplifying themselves to fatherliness with elaborate backpacks and juice boxes in hand), he always thought, *Who are you trying to impress?* But here he was, looking back at himself (this girl on his shoulders, amazed at being almost as high as the aeroplanes, *Who are you trying to impress?*) when the sound of a lawnmower, wasping the smell of cut grass over the garden fences, made Michael feel ashamed. He found it hard to believe the dandelions between the paving slabs were his.

While the kids played funerals, burying their sticks, Michael played a game with the back of Esme's head he called *What's on the front of Esme's head?* It had only taken him a week or so since waking up to learn that a ponytail meant she was catching up with work; she was probably chewing her lip and wincing – like she had in the hospital, while he was stranded and hoping she'd leave the room. Hers was the first face he saw and his memory of it was smeared. Whenever he thought of the deprivation, of forgetting, say, your entire marriage, he just laughed: it was hard to care about the loss of something you could never remember. Hard to bear the loss of the only thing you could. He couldn't even bury his dog in the garden, do things properly. Suppose she lost her life (what gains it?): they'd make him walk to the front of the service in a dark suit, slug-glints of kid-snot on his sleeve, and remember her. This woman, who seemed so kind and intelligent, who'd sat at his bedside while he was absolutely nowhere to be seen, who'd waited for him, who'd invested herself in him, committed herself to him: he had lost her life. Not all of it; he didn't think that much of himself. Enough of it. Enough of this almost stranger, who'd held his hands, for the first time, out of his hospital bed – as he looked over his shoulder to see the white, pulled-back sheets and the indentation he'd been, and felt unmade.

But when he stepped into the house for *another* coffee and saw her rubbing her temples, frustrated at something on the computer, he remembered coming back from the farm off the main road and back to this kitchen, back to her still stressing about the exhibition she was helping to curate, back in the days when she helped to curate (all he'd heard for weeks, months, was *Maximian . . . Maximian . . . Maximian . . .*), surprising her with a pile of fur in his hand.

Say hello to Maximian!

She crouched down on to the floor with him, nearly crying at the smallness of the fur nosing and padding from her palms, the almost impossible delicacy of something ever being alive – and Louis said, *What's wrong Mummy?* then *Wow!* as he fingertipped his fur back so the dog's black eyes came peeping out.

He wanted to run to her and, shaking her shoulders and hugging her, shout *I remember you! I remember you!*

Esme, he said, feeling sudden and now in the room, among the leftover hot-dog buns, the briny tin, the dirty cups and the breadcrumbed plates with ketchup stains that ought to be in the dishwasher.

Yeah? she asked, looking up at his sudden face, his halted face, sweetly.

Where's the sweetener?

He'd failed. Michael went back to his chair. There was nothing else of her that he could remember. There was Esme with the puppy. There was Esme in the hospital. Two magnetic norths repulsing against his mind's attempt to bring things together.

He gave up. Let the garden chair carry him through an afternoon of busy sunlight, of reading the news on the phone, of trying to ignore the two little voices winding around him, of enough insects fussing the flowers to make you think that nothing was wrong.

Mara, shouted Louis tetchily, you've got to hide properly.

She was balancing on her tiptoes on the edge of the wall, daydreaming beneath the sound of the sky taking off and landing, that ocean of motorway just over the horizon, flies hurling themselves at the windows; the more he listened to the garden, the more everything felt urgent and confused.

Mara! You're not playing!

Now here he was in this garden, his shadow cooling its head on the grass. His children's shadows mingling with the shadows of the house and the fence and the flowers. Children who tugged his sleeve and said *Daddy*, as though they hadn't confused him with someone else. Whether he loved them or not, he felt tacky trying to make them love him, needily wanting them to love him – saying to himself, *You sad bastard*, when he smiled or tried to make them laugh. It was better to stay in this chair, not looking up from his phone, detached, cynical, without loss. (He remembered sitting here: Louis and the dog playing on the grass, the dog laughing, the boy barking, wrestling each other from each other.) The inextricableness of it all nagged him, though: him, them. Maybe he was supposed to be here, with the kids growing up in the garden and the rosebuds threatening to open, everything pushing itself apart.

Maybe, but it was easier to remind himself of Esme's persistent fretting and cautioning, the boy's tedious know-it-all-ness, the girl's mood swings – to remind himself, when he crouched to play with the kids, *You sad bastard*. To be none of it. Sit in the garden staring at his phone, his head in the football scores, and not expect to feel that yelp in his gut because Mara had screamed.

But Mara had screamed.

She was his child. The sight was in his head before he turned to see it: on the slabs, doll-flat, one arm back to front, hair clotting in the blood on her forehead. The totality of it, suddenly – the way he'd turn her as gently as his panic could manage, her disjointed little body, there being no way of holding her that made her look quite right. This vivid, lifeless image: all this in an instant, and when he turned: there she was,

Mara?

standing on the patio as if it had never happened.

*

He ran to her. She was still.

Mara – what happened? Are you OK?

She shrugged as if she didn't know what he was talking about. He heard her fall. The thud of it; unmistakable.

Did you fall? What? Did she fall, Louis?

Louis looked at him with that way kids have of making you feel as though you've missed something completely obvious about the world. The boy drifted back to throwing the ball up into the tree, giggling as it tumbled through the branches.

Mara. Mara!

She was already skittering towards the house. He looked at the patio, expecting blood.

What's the matter? Esme called from the back door, a cold sweat at her wine glass.

Nothing, he said. Nothing.

A weird thought occurred to Michael.

Which was how he found himself standing in the middle of the lawn that night with a brick in his hand. He'd managed to hold out until everyone had gone to bed, pretending he was staying up to watch the football highlights (clever ruse: presumably pre-coma Michael behaviour). Now he was alone with the night lights and the occasional dog far off, barking at nothing.

The brick looked aggravated, a sunburnt forehead. But its weight had a cool earthiness to it. He composed himself. Balanced from foot to foot. Bats bluffed their thicker darkness at the edges of the garden, eating the insects that were just then bombarding the security lights. He stayed still enough to trick them into his absence.

To prove to himself that he hadn't lost his mind, that his weird thought might not be so weird, he threw the brick as hard as he could at his foot. Imagined the crack of the bone, the raw shock. And when he opened his eyes, there was the brick, squatting idly beside his uninjured foot.

Just as he'd feared.

He hadn't missed. He couldn't have missed.

★

A moth touched by; he flinched.

He'd do it again. Now with his eyes open – but again, really concentrating on the brick hitting his foot. This time he threw it much harder. The shot that would smash his foot – he pictured an excruciating, direct shot – didn't. Somehow the path of the brick moved, or his foot moved, or the world moved, or—. He didn't know.

I definitely didn't stop it from busting my foot just by imagining it, he whispered to himself. I definitely didn't stop Mara from smashing her head.

His solid assurances misted into night air.

This was stupid – it was too easy to miss his foot. There'd be something else that had got in the way, something unconscious guiding his hand. No – he'd throw it upwards and align his head with the brick's plummet. Hope that it wouldn't leave him with the humiliating gash he'd imagined before the throw. Or would, maybe. He didn't know what to hope.

Through his closed lids he saw the security lights come on – they must have caught the flight of the brick, slung from his hand and hurling its corners towards his skull.

He panicked and jumped out of the way.

The brick thumped the grass sickeningly. It looked at him, disgusted.

Michael breathed carefully. Being hit on the head is no fuss, he reassured himself: you just disappear from yourself.

Again, holding the brick, thinking of the brick – of the thing lobbed above his head in the night-yellow garden and of it smashing him on the head – he held his breath and let the brick go up, high enough to give him time to line himself underneath it.

A yelp: a timid, reflux yelp. And a sickener of a thud.

Touching the top of his head, he was sure there was a gash there, raw and hot in the cool night – but his fingers found nothing. A bat-shriek laugh let loose before his hand slapped his mouth shut. When he dared open his eyes he saw the brick, beside him. He'd been directly beneath it. It should have put him out of his misery, smashed him back into a coma. Or better.

Delicately he stepped away from it, in case it changed its mind.

OK, he sighed.

Crouching down to where the brick lay on the floor, he smiled inviolably at its dumb weight, concentrating on its compact simplicity, the way its grain textured some subtlety into the security lights' glare. Eyes closed, concentrated on it as completely as he could.

The brick that sat in his mind vanished from his eyes.

He sprang up. Looked around, hand over mouth – no one had seen, had they?

The houses were all dark. No bird-eyed glint in the trees. Just daft moths at the garden lights. The mist of his hyperventilating through his damp fingers.

He – no, it was ridiculous, only someone who'd lost their grip would think it – had vanished the brick by imagining it.

He tried not to laugh. It came out like a cough.

Without so much as a change in the light, the world thinned – it seemed to have such a slight grasp on itself. As though everything was floating on the surface of its own disappearance. It was a weirdly natural feeling, the way he supposed a salmon feels magnetic fields through the foil of its body, or a dolphin hears pregnancy's heartbeats: he could sense the nothing of things. Only small things, for now, maybe, but by touching the completeness of something he could bring it to its absence. If he could focus enough, though, he reckoned he could make the fence vanish, the shed, maybe something as complicated as a tree – screw it, he could probably undo the entire house, the street. All it took was a certain concentration to make a nowhere of the here and now.

Michael smirked, glancing around: everything had to justify itself to him.

His vanishings were random. He studied things about the place, anything; pictured them. Gone. Twigs, leaves. A flat football. A doll lodged in the lower boughs of the tree (this took a few goes: body first, hair, head, then last its eyes, floating by the leaves). Nothing remained.

If anyone nearby had woken for a piss and found themselves at their window, their attention caught by the lights in the backyard one or two doors down, they'd have seen – *Is that?* – Michael, scuttling from spot to spot in his garden, stopping to stare at something, as though he'd seen a mole or a snail or maybe a nose of honey fungus, something indecipherable from this far – inspecting, then pointing, amazed, or holding his head in his hands, and running to the next spot, again – before they sloped back to bed, carrying the thought of the poor bloke who was knocked into a coma by a freak golf shot, having a tough time of it in his garden.

⋆

Then an almost anxious thought touched the back of his neck, an unease. He held out his empty hand.

Imagined the brick not existing.

When he opened his eyes, there was still nothing.

Fuck, he said. It's not coming back.

The dark upstairs of her house watched over him. As if he'd go upstairs with his news and she wouldn't lock the kids in the bathroom while he protested (*the brick!*), trying to keep him downstairs with a soothing voice until the emergency services arrived with their cool injection into his bicep. But, there was this compulsion: boyishly to sprint up the stairs, to tell her right now, on only the second night he could remember spending in her bed, with the light still breaking into her eyes, to show her what he could do, what they could do—

Michael stood indecisively still; the security lights burst into papery wings. All across the garden the moony scribble of slugs. He sighed. His shadows lengthened from the house.

23

That Sunday morning landed on his head like a ton of—. In bed, with a wife he barely knew, their youngest crawling through the sheets and the unspeakable anxiety of what happened in the garden last night.

Michael snailed about the house, thinking of Max. Thinking that he'd imagined his daughter falling and she hadn't. That he'd imagined a brick and it had vanished. That he'd imagined his dog loping towards him, licking his face, barking its big, daft bark, and it hadn't. No one could tease him out from under his own thoughts. The kids, with their canine sense for the preternatural, were straight to the garden, wagging outside of themselves. Louis stood on the patchy grass, his hair nerving some change; Mara went nosing about the bushes. He was the culprit at the window, watching police comb the reeds.

But there's only so long they can stop the flood of their kiddishness; Louis found another flat football and began scoring past the ghost in the small goal, shouting at Mara to watch – Mara, whose twig-wand was casting spells (*Nothung!*) on the magpies to turn them into chickens.

Esme left the back door open (meekly hoping the mouse would leave and not return). Kids were blowing through the house – mostly the two he recognised.

Bad head, he winced, when Esme asked if he was OK. All day he lay on the sofa with that slouching, peripheral thunder of a headache never quite breaking clear – sulking there, brought on (he worried) by all the heat of his imaginings.

If Esme noticed anything was missing from the garden, she didn't mention it. Her silence was his guilt. *Dogs run away*, he kept repeating to himself. Even happy dogs. Suppose Max missed him, and was looking for him. He could've fallen down ~~a mine shaft~~, ~~a sink hole~~, ~~a mysterious vortex~~ . . . A storm drain, maybe. Sometimes strangers steal dogs – that was plausible. It was more plausible than the thought that he'd imagined Max out of existence. But dog theft – it just felt less true. He stared at the white walls, at the TV. Tried to keep everything exactly where it was. Prevented anything from entering his mind that could vanish outside of it.

When the house went quiet, when he couldn't hear anyone, the panic rose. Had he? If he'd vanished the dog, then . . . He didn't dare set out of the room to look. But it was there. The thick, anxious heart of his throat. Thickening into his breath: *what if . . . what if . . . what if . . .*

Then one of them would pop their head in the room, see him lying with the blanket up to his eyes and smile. No, he hadn't vanished a child. The low note could begin again, rising.

★

A fly broke in, making a moron of itself against the window, against the walls. He was anxious to imagine it because it couldn't really vanish; he was anxious not to imagine it, because what if it did?

Every now and then Esme would float in with a glass of water, touch him on the shoulder and ask him,

D'you want a cup of tea, yet?

while

Mara hefted up his arm, letting it slap on his belly.

You're so silly, Daddy. You might get stuck again.

Mostly they left him alone in the living room.

Exhausted, the fly landed near Michael, cleaning itself. He caught it, dozy, under his empty glass. Now it was panicking. Aiming elsewhere – not there – not there. He wondered what it felt like: to take off and find the air sudden and solid. Everything warped through the curvature. Its grease marks on the air. It conceded. Or forgot. Climbed the wall of the glass. Stopped. Washed the muck from its legs with short swipes through its mouth. Continued.

While he was trying to hold it in his mind without losing it, he said, a little too loud,

You're losing it, Michael.

But everything was the same as always, more or less.

It grew dark before he noticed, still laid out on the sofa.

Night night, Daddy.

Michael wasn't watching some gardening programme when Louis came downstairs, showing off his clean smell and fresh pyjamas, trailing Mr Leonard by his plush toy-dog ears. The boy crawled into his armpit, walking his fingers up his dad's arm as though they were a little man's legs discovering a mountain, singing his little-man walking song.

Doopeedoopeedoo.

Feeling the two small prints on the outcrop of his skin, Michael had to swallow to stop himself from crying: so thoughtlessly close to him, and he could barely remember the boy at all. With his free hand he rubbed his eyes. But he must have moved too much, because – *Ah no! Waaaaaaaaaah!* – the little man fell from up by Michael's ear, crashing and scrawling all the way down. He lay splatted on Michael's thigh.

Bleurgh. I'll have to start again now.

And the little man kicked his legs. Sprang upright. Began trekking up the leg when—

Louis! Storytime!

Esme shouted. Louis clambered down from the sofa and out of the room, dragging Mr Leonard behind him, paws outstretched, polished eyes pleading at Michael, being dragged from the room.

Michael felt a coldness on his chest; Louis' damp hair had left a print on his T-shirt.

It was dry by the time Esme came downstairs.

What you watching?

I'm not, really.

She sat down beside him; leaned over for the remote. Found an episode of one of those programmes she liked where they dig up parts of the countryside in the hope of discovering something that wouldn't make it on to telly if it hadn't been buried first.

D'you mind? she asked.

He shrugged.

They didn't talk. As though they were engrossed in the excavation of an imperial outpost near a motorway bypass.

While he was trying to think of a way to tell his newly discovered spouse that he'd stopped her daughter from falling, imagined a brick out of existence, and perhaps also his dog, Esme slumped across the sofa, taking his hands in hers, pressing her head up against his belly.

She stayed there. Cumbersomely.

(He remembered when he was just a teenager and Siobhan put her head in his lap at the cinema and neither of them knew what to do next, so while she got a crick in her neck from the armrest he stroked her head, as though she was a cat.)

Michael didn't touch his wife.

I've got something! shouted a squat, bearded man in a trench.

Desperately keeping himself in the present tense, Michael was trying to construct a sentence explaining that he wasn't out of his mind, but . . .

Esme sighed melodramatically.

What's up?

He was terrified of what she'd say, but it was impolite not to ask.

She rose, tried to make eye contact with him.

Are you in a mood with me?

Uh?

I – you've just been. I dunno, it seems like since the other day you've been upset with me. Since we got home. Have I done something wrong?

No.

So you're not in a mood with me?

I barely – look, I'm still just a bit overwhelmed by everything.

She nuzzled up to his arm, ran her fingers through his hair.

I'm sorry, she said. I shouldn't have said anything.

Uneasily, she leaned on him. Uneasy, he tried not to make himself comfortable.

There's a whole load of them, said the beard in the trench. *I think we've found a wall, Trish!*

I thought you were dead.

What?

She was crying. He was startled.

Gone. You were gone. You left me alone.

The unfinished fear of it all thrummed through her: the shock, the waiting, the nothingness, the leadenness, the responsibility for that body, the loss of the one person she'd want to help her in dealing with it. She'd looked at him in the hospital bed and seen not just a man she loved being drip-fed and monitored, but so much of herself, too; the way it was to be her when he spoke to her, when he touched her, when he looked at her or thought about her, the things they'd done together, the life she would live in him, that the kids would live in him. Finally, she was crying for it. Not the nervous, frustrated tears of the hospital – something totally exhausted, utterly clear.

He should have mentioned his imagination undoing things, he thought, got it in while she was weak. It was too late now. And far too late to tell her that it was a tad awkward, her being so intimate like this, because he still wasn't entirely sure who she was. So he stared at the TV.

Kevin has made an exciting discovery: what appears to be an outer wall running through the eastern trench. Could this be the house we were looking for?

And she was too much. Shuddering. Wiping snot from her face. Even though he was probably mentally ill and wouldn't be much of a husband anyway, going around thinking he could imagine things out of existence. It was laughable. The thought of them walking in the park; him pointing at things that weren't there, her smiling, holding his hand.

You were so shallow, she continued, lying down,

intubated. This awful breath noise. It was like you'd been half-eaten by some machine.

She must have felt it flulp in his belly – looked up. He'd turned away, biting his lip.

Are you laughing?

She leaned back across the sofa.

No, he said.

He stood up before she could interrogate him any further. Mumbled something about a drink, taking the upturned glass with him. Hand over his mouth, the laughter spurting through his fingers.

By the sink, he laughed under the sound of the running water – a breathy, hysterical laugh. It seemed ridiculous. He was here, disaster averted! Besides, there was almost nothing to lose. His miraculous reincarnation, midway through a tedious life as an insurance-something-or-other in a commuter town . . . It didn't exactly seem worth dying for.

Listening to her footsteps ascending the stairs to bed, he took a few deep and stuttering breaths. With the laughter sore at the back of his throat, he downed the long, cool glass of water. Wiped his mouth dry with a short swipe of his forearm. Then, as quietly as he could, began to cry.

22

It only took a few days for everyone to return to their normal lives. Esme was back at work; Louis was at school; Mara, nursery. And Michael, who was barricaded in a house, trying to convince himself he couldn't imagine things out of existence. That later, his wife and children would could home and he'd know exactly who they were.

He was trying to postpone the normal life they had planned for him, underemployed in the insurance industry. It was his fate; the swipe card on his bedside table said so. But he had no idea what he'd done wrong to qualify for such a job. Or even what the hell people *in insurance* actually do. All he could recall was the detuned-television pattern of the carpet tiles. The stack of replacements they kept in the store cupboard. What workplace allowances do they have to make for a man who thinks he can erase things using only his mind? You can't just retrofit a ramp. They'd all have to go to a *sensitivity training day* at a conference centre off a motorway, working through exercises where they pretended to imagine things out of existence and brainstorming a word cloud about how it feels to vanish things. In the breaks they'd vape outside by the sodden verge while the lorries barged past and he'd try to make 'normal' conversation, even though they'd all been dragged out here for a big fuss over his little brain-thing.

No – he would stay at home and be nothing special. To make him feel useful, less of an invalid, Esme had asked him to lay a trap for the mouse. It was one of those humane ones, like a wiretap or capitalism. The mouse walked happily into the box, as though it really believed in free will. Michael looked at the white walls of the house and shivered. On his way to release it in the woods, he smiled and waved to the woman across the road as she loaded two Irish setters into her car – delighted at himself for having a secret mouse in his bag.

Automatically, he found himself on his old dog-walking route: down the scutty path behind the estate, along the edge of the golf course and into the remainder of the woods, clenched between the town and the motorway. He'd lost his granddad, a friend and countless goldfish: all griefs that had visited him from the amnesia of his coma. He remembered coffins, elegies, cold sausage rolls. The goldfish – flushed down the toilet bowl on the second go – barely seemed alive in the first place. Things that can't remember much don't have to worry about being much remembered. Animals drop through the trapdoor of their shadow into nothing. But dogs, though. Dogs are half-peopled: they eat in the kitchen, sleep in front of the TV. Dogs don't just disappear, they go missing. Once (he was sure) Esme asked him *If you could be anyone, who would you be?* and he pointed at his dog. Their dog – who was right there, first thing, sniffing over his thoughts when he stopped being so bloody comatose.

Get over it! he said to himself. *You came back from the dead, and you're fixated on a fucking dog!* This was the furthest he'd walked, feeble-limbed from six supine weeks. The path had forked off severally without him really noticing. Paths that warped with each step, their canopy implying weather with a stray drop or splotch. Late light fell from leaf to leaf down to the fag packets and cans, mossy tyres and other tidemarks of the town. Down to the smell of leaf mould and fox piss. A cascade of church bells, near-distance, in all directions. At some point, a jogger approached with that jogger's concern on their face – passed with a splash of music, a nod – as though he was any other person. Michael pretended to be looking for his dog, who had just run off into the woods, rather than not looking for his dog, who had not just run off into the woods.

And now he'd been walking for a while and this overgrown industrial site, fenced in at the edge of the field, was unfamiliar. He didn't even recognise the field. The map on his phone was a grid of blank space.

Bastard, he said.

This was supposed to be the place he'd grown up. It was supposed to be the place he lived.

Three times he tried redoubling his steps; three times he returned to this spot.

The low-sunned shadows thatched into each other. He panicked. Imagined himself stuck out here for days, foraging for berries and (the great hope) a stray Mars bar left in the Portakabin over that fence.

Max! he shouted.

If anyone found him, at least it would appear as though he was looking for his dog. But this holloway could go fuck itself. And that stump. The mulch. The birds – don't get him started on the birds. Arseholes. (He was walking quickly now, hobbling, his breath chuffing off into the near-dark.) What was she doing, this Esme, leaving him at home unsupervised, as if nothing had happened? She at least ought to have locked him in. (He remembered her laughing hysterically from the other side of the glass, holding the key – him trapped in her backyard, naked [why was he naked?!], and thumping *Esme! Esme!* on the door, which only agitated the security light. They were almost still kids, really. When she eventually let him in, he shouted *What the fuck's the matter with you?* because it was only a joke, because she was so intelligent, and so funny, and so pretty, because this made him feel like he was a pathetic, naked man who could be exiled to the backyard, banging on her door to be let in. Because she had let him in.) And there –

Lights! The familiar, distant motorway lapping over the sound of his wheeze like a sea. Nearby, the old village mouldered over the stream. Michael slowed to a limp (his knees!). Coughed. The holloway gave him back up to the lane without a dog.

Floodlights lit white the driving range behind the fence. Between the stray cars you'd hear, every now and then, the faint thock of a lone, late golfer testing their stroke. It was here – near here, Michael thought – the incident. He searched for the exact spot, half-crouching on the night-grey grass beside the path.

There wasn't a trace. Nothing came back to him. Indifferent grass, indifferent flagstones, indifferent road. He lay down almost in the gauze of the street lamp, in the chill prickle of the grass, its damp seeping into his jeans.

The last time he lay down here he had a family. Now he was a man in a family. With no dog. Shrunken. Elsewhere. (He wondered how the mouse felt, as he set it down, frightening off into the undergrowth.) Waiting for some giant hands to carry him away.

Back home that evening, Michael avoided the family – pretending to tidy his shed. So Louis pretended to play in the garden, edging towards his dad. Loudly finding *amazing* things and asking semi-rhetorical questions. Michael wasn't so numb as to not sense the boy trying to find the courage to talk to him – just numb enough to be scared of risking some emotional connection by talking. Soon it was bathtime; Michael was still in his shed, rummaging for courage.

When something brought Esme, blurred, to the yellow window looking out on her husband, she found him a few steps closer, standing in a daze on the grass. His four faint shadows, folded moth wings, imbricated behind him by the security lights on the lawn; at least, he thought, I'm not completely alone. She seemed more certain of him than he did. He trusted that when she saw him, she saw something that stretched further back in time than the man who had woken up in a hospital bed about a fortnight ago. He'd loved her once. Maybe he could love her again.

★

He smiled up at her. It was hard to tell through the blurry window, but he thought she smiled back. As though she could see him in full health again, playing in the backyard with the kids and the dog.

Except they had no dog.

Esme, he said.

She came downstairs from putting the kids to bed to find near-darkness and him in the blue light of the hob, stirring chicken soup. There was bread on the table. Invalid food.

Smells nice, she said, rubbing her belly. The Minotaur's growling.

The fuse must have tripped again, because the oven clock was flashing 00:00. Just as she was about to turn towards the fuse box beneath the stairs, he said:

I lost Max.

Who?

I disappeared him.

OK, she said.

If he hadn't been crying, showing her around the things he'd done in the garden, she looked as though she might have laughed. He'd mumbled incoherently in the kitchen – pointed out where Mara hadn't fallen (*Landed!*) – the flat football that wasn't down the side of the shed (*Vanished!*), the doll that wasn't stuck in the tree (*Gone!*) – and had picked up a loose brick from the garden wall (that really needed fixing) and was about to throw it at his foot when she said,

No! Michael. I believe you.

I just picture it and—

I know, she said. It undoes.

Undoes: that didn't sound quite right. He didn't quite believe her.

She hugged him – almost as though she was trying to stop him talking – then led him back into the house, where the low flame of the hob was spitting chicken soup at the tiles.

Her placidity unnerved him. This all seemed too familiar to her. Too easy. He reckoned the coma must have hollowed her, possibly. All this – she was unmoved. Or not exactly unmoved. Distant. The way the sea is distant in the ear of a conch (he remembered his little head on his auntie's chest on the way back from the beach, sleepy as kelp). The way his old life approached and receded from so far away. In the certain light of the fridge, she looked unsure.

What are you after?

She reached out a hand towards him without looking – or a part of her did, a quieter part.

The spread, she answered.

For the first time he could remember since coming home, he was holding her hand. But holding her hand felt like holding a hand she was holding.

They dipped slices of bread in the insipid soup while he used words like *miracle* and *Max* and *oblivion* and *damned-if-I-know.* She nodded vaguely along. Those not-so-sly glances at her phone indicated that she had work in the morning. He could imagine things out of existence; what the hell was wrong with her?

When she brushed her teeth, she locked the bathroom door. He hoped, at least, to hear her sobbing. Or cursing him. Or stabbing the walls with her toothbrush. Anything that would give her away. Not even the sound of her peeing betrayed her. She came to bed smiling tenderly, as if he'd bumped his knee. Seemed to go to sleep without any trouble.

For most of the night Michael stared at the back of his eyelids.

21

It went on for days; at breakfast, Esme avoided his eyes. Shadowed the kids. Laughed loudly. He couldn't tell if she was protecting them or they were protecting her. The kitchen air was rich with milk and Rice Krispies and was no place to talk about imagining things out of existence. While he was scraping the leftovers into the bin she made it out of the door to work with a child in each hand. The blurred shape he saw in the frosted glass had barely said goodbye.

Although he could recount the facts – golf ball, coma, woke up weird – Michael still wasn't quite sure how he'd arrived here. The quiet house estranged him with his noises. His footsteps on the floorboards. His piss in the bowl. Everything in the house was goading him to vanish it. It made him anxious. He had to stop himself. Anything could be a clue. The penny jar. Used batteries. The clothes recycling bag for the charity shop in the kitchen drawer. He didn't remember himself having so much willpower.

Tidying up after the kids, folding clothes away, lining toys neatly. It was almost therapeutic, placing them back into order like that. They'd textured everything, the house thick with kid: wall marks, frayings, brokenness. Rubbing Mara's greasy handprint from the mirror in her room, he remembered watching Louis first meet her (Louis, who commandeered language like a conquistador, who crushed *Flowers!* in his hand out of admiration, who ripped out his daddy's *Hair!* gleefully, who knocked *Joe!* over because he was so glad to see him) – his fingers on the soft top of her head so softly it would leave no impression on the word *touch*. His son; his daughter.

Being in their rooms without them felt as though it was a trap: any second one would spring out of their cupboard, the other climb out from under their bed, shouting *Daddy's rubbish at staying awake!*

Then he panicked – her fingerprints, cleaned from the mirror, it felt so final (she'd only mucky it again, but . . .). The thought that he could inadvertently vanish even something so little as a bobble splayed with Mara's hairs or a mud-scut from Louis' trainers was squashing his head.

So Esme would come home to find him in this sort of mood. He wondered why she wasn't working from home, whether she was only going to the office to avoid him. To avoid these awkward encounters with the strange man who'd woken up inside her husband's body, who'd once claimed that he could imagine things out of existence and was now staring at her over a plate of fish fingers, chips and peas as though he wanted her to ask, *How's your day been, love? Vanish anything interesting?*

When they spoke, they spoke about barely anything at all.

20

Against his protests, Esme drove him to the doctor's appointment. He must have looked nervous, because she held his hand as they walked across the car park into the reception, and every now and then squeezed his thigh comfortingly in the waiting room. Its magazines had saddened at the edges and the morning's rain shower steamed from coats in a fug of worry.

While the doctor went through the usual questions (headaches, dizziness, disorientation), Michael kept trying to sneak a glance at his scan, expecting there might be some black acorn buried in his brain, a branching absence.

And you've still no memory of the accident itself? she asked.

Nope.

But he narrowed his eyes at her, trying to make himself look suspicious in his flippancy. If the doctor could intuit that he'd imagined the dog out of existence, that would be satisfying from a diagnostic viewpoint. Tell them, and he's a lunatic; let them uncover it, he's a medical marvel. Just some confirmation. Any sort of confirmation.

OK Michael. Well, I think you're progressing really well.

They were all smiles and goodbyes. Until, shuffling her bag back on to her shoulder, Esme asked the doctor if she could have a quick word – nudging him out of the door with a nervous glance.

He stood in the corridor. Huffily. (He was such a push-over. Why didn't he stay there, unbudged?) Listening to their muffled voices. Trying to keep his glances through the door's slim window inconspicuous. A moustached man Michael didn't recognise smiled and nodded at him; he pretended he hadn't seen him. The eyes of the waiting room grew like a mole on the back of his neck. He kept glancing at the door as he pretended to read the news about a factory closure on his phone.

He might have known Esme once. He didn't really know her now. Didn't know how she would take news like his. They were talking about him, Esme and the doctor – he was sure. Conspiring. She'd be telling the doctor how he wasn't the man she'd rushed to hospital for. He'd come back a sullen man. A mean man. Delusional. Thinking he could erase things with his mind. That this wasn't her husband, lurking on the corridor. His brain was addled. He needed institutionalising.

Some nerve, he muttered to himself, sounding unnervingly like his father.

Esme clicked out on to the corridor all lightness, mid-laughter, giving her goodbyes as she closed the door to the doctor's office. She led him confidently from the waiting room, skirting the workman botching up a broken door with some hazard tape.

A wordless walk back through the hospital: dodging beds, porters, crutches with people grown on to them. Michael huffed, trying not to accost her here, now. They got lost in the corridors, twice, before the bright air pushed it out of him in the car park.

What the hell was all that about?

Esme was taken aback.

What were you saying about me?

Oh, we were just talking about you being the centre of the universe.

She tried to laugh him away, but he said:

Esme—

sternly.

Birds clamped on to the gutters, the lamp posts, listening in. An ambulance came flashing into the bay without its siren on.

Do you think I'm mad? D'you think I need to see someone?

She hesitated, as though she wasn't entirely sure if he was challenging her or asking to be looked after. In the space she left he started to well up.

Michael—

He batted her hand away before she could touch his arm.

No, it's fine. You obviously think I'm delusional. So—

Michael, no. I—

Standing too close to the ambulance bay, they were interrupted by the burst of the doors; the patient, his oxygen mask slung rakishly, hyphenated into an awkward marital heart-to-heart in the car park.

Esme offered a *get well soon* smile to the man being lowered from the ambulance. Or what she thought passed for one.

They sank towards the car, struggling to know what to say. He paused by the door. The apprehension of its enclosed space, a new(ish) wife who thought he was delirious, maybe – he couldn't. It was the humiliation of it. Wondering the whole way home which one of the two of them believed he could imagine things from existence, which one was going to get him committed.

Come on, Michael.

She sighed into the seat, unsure of herself. Put her seatbelt on. And there, the sight of her, the seatbelt – he felt a sudden halt in the world: imagined her clashing through the windscreen on to the road, broken glass speckling her cuts.

We need to pick Mara up.

She sounded on edge, but he didn't respond. He touched the roof of the car, sunk in the thought of her on the road. Of how paused, how stupefied he'd be at the loss. The weight of her loss. The unequal force of the world against his need to lift her and carry her safely away.

Michael—. Come on, let's get Mara and go home.

Even if he knew almost none of it, the half-lit recesses of their life together, he asked himself if what he felt at the thought of her sprawled on the road, that horror, was the impression of love.

He sat beside her. (Remembered them getting up in a field, a little faint, the flattened grass beginning to awake from beneath them.)

I wasn't . . . She was trying not to sound snappy. I was just thanking the doctor for looking after you.

He nodded, as though he understood. The engine was impatient. His door closed with a secure click.

The rest of the day passed in a truce, kept well to each other's borders.

I'm going to bed, said Esme.

OK, said Michael, I'm just gonna watch this.

Another action film about the end of the world. When the credits arrived and everything was (destruction aside) back to normal, he stepped out into the garden to listen to the plants breathe. It lit up like a crime scene at his movement. He imagined this shed wrestled down by ivy. Trees prising apart the bricks of this house. Wild deer ghosting through the overgrowth. He picked up Mara's hand-me-down toy car from where it had crash-landed beneath the begonia and his vision of Esme bleeding on the road returned. The car was cold in his hand. It felt like it would survive.

Esme, he said, quietly. Esme.

When she woke up, he was standing in the dim of their bedroom holding another brick.

What? Michael?

Peering in the dark, but also with a *What is it with you and bricks?* look on her face. The way she made a question of his name relit the nerves he'd managed to cool with some deep breaths in the dark. He was about to explain that they had so many leftovers in the shed from the small wall he'd built (he remembered Louis pestering him in the cement-sweaty day for an ice cream from the van) when Esme said,

Michael.

Her voice a soft hand on his chest, as though he'd woken from troubled sleep – that everything was fine. For a moment he doubted himself; then

Esme, I'm gonna put the light on.

She sat up with an anguished squint.

Michael—

She held a hand out for him, inviting him into bed. He held out the brick.

I'm going to vanish this.

Michael, please—

I need you to see it, Esme.

Please, Michael, come on – come to bed.

The blanket pulled back, the sheet's creased warmth.

I need you to believe me, Esme.

I do, I—

He closed his eyes – settled into the headspace where he could concentrate on the brick, on vanishing the brick. The brick in his mind. The rough heft of it. And felt the weight of it lift from his hands.

When he opened his eyes, Esme had placed her palms in his, lightly guiding him into bed. He resisted.

Do you?

She nodded, bitten-lipped.

Really?

Still nodding, reeling him gently into bed, the tense exhaustion crashed through his limbs. She smothered the duvet over their heads, tangled her arms in his arms. *She believes me*, he kept thinking, as his wife kissed his neck, comfortingly, as though she really believed him.

A car door closed down the road. He wasn't sure when she'd untangled herself. The light was off. When did he go to sleep? He thought he could hear her crying, and when he turned to see, the tide of her breath was slack.

19

In the morning, they carried on like parents in a cereal advert. He wasn't sure if he ought to be worried at how easily they could pretend all was right with the world. The kids were throwing teddies at each other, arguing about whether Mara's friend could read Louis' thoughts or not and Esme was laughing along, filming them, which infuriated him. (They seemed completely oblivious to being filmed.) And just as the frustration of going on as though nothing had ever happened was threatening to surface, she dragged him into the cupboard beneath the stairs.

The place stank of old walks and vacuum dust. He had to fold himself half a dozen times to fit.

Right, she said. So.

She offered terms; he'd come to her defeated, pointing at bricks that didn't exist, telling her he'd vanished the dog, that he'd stopped her daughter falling. Their daughter.

This is how it goes, she said.

Gesticulating to his forehead, repeatedly, she explained that whatever was going on in there, they could handle it. *But this doesn't leave the house.* She seemed so composed, so alert, maybe even a little weirdly energised by the whole thing. He'd imagined her getting him committed in a teary scene in the living room, the kids peeking down through the banister as he's led from the house by stab-proof vests. Had he imagined her into this reaction? He didn't think he could really do that; maybe she did. *OK*, he nodded while she explained how things would work, *OK*. Prohibitions, strict routines, *under control*. Her eyes were wide. She kept jabbing his chest, as though it was supposed to motivate him; it felt as though it would leave a mark. When it seemed like she was almost done, she said something half-joking about making himself useful and pulled from her pocket a piece of folded paper.

Imagine these, she said.

It was a list. She must have written it before he woke up, before the kids were up, in the quiet house – that slight bruise of chill that comes just before a sunrise, the pipes coughing like milkmen, dew on the cobwebs. He hated that hour.

He looked it over, his face scrunched.

I—

She put her finger to his mouth, kissed him and held him.

We're going to be OK, she said. This is all going to be fucking OK. I love you.

With another small kiss on the cheek, she left him alone in the cupboard.

Although he could see the logic, he wasn't going to do it. He thought about going out – made it as far as putting his shoes on. Stood at the door, holding the handle. He was trying to remember bringing Louis home – stairs, tables, sharp objects, dull objects, food, water, air, everything about their life then felt like a death trap. He could just about remember the swaddled boy. The swaddled girl. And felt less like he'd helped bring them into the world than guard them against it: he was a closed door, with two little pairs of hands trying to push him aside, eyes peeping through at the keyhole. Maybe he could, at some point, eventually, stop worrying.

Esme seemed less anxious, having already funnelled Louis through the catastrophe that is childbirth. But his anxieties must have stretched their nerves into her, sharpened the edges of their home. The staircase loomed; he remembered them on fox feet upstairs one night, the sickly airlessness, the panic. Leaning over his cot in the dark room: *I can't – can you?!* The anxious backs of their hands wavered above him for the touch of his breath. *Should we wake him up?!* This was what they got for all the complaints about his crying. This was parental karma. Ears lowered to the sleep of their boy: listening for his breathlessness in the dark as though they were listening for the end of the world. (He was breathing. He was fine. It was nothing.) And realising that it would never stop. That this was them, now. This amputated nausea, this separation anxiety – even when the kids were there – say, by a road, in a crowd, all alone: the cut of that thought – *Is Louis OK? Is Mara OK?*

But drowsing around the house for the rest of the day, that refrain: *I'd only make things worse.* So when Esme returned with two sleepy kids and cornered him on the landing to ask,

Have you?

he was pretending he had a headache and also that he didn't hear her, and that if he did hear he didn't know what she was on about.

He opened his mouth and—

It turned out that all he needed was for her to accept that his brain had changed; only needed her to believe in the version of the world that he did. To feel (even if there was so much of her that was still missing in him) that they were here together. That even if their *here* was unreal, the *there* they'd abandoned was really the same. Now they could go back to their life prior to the golf ball's intrusion. The coma, the moods, the rest of it – they could bury that and be the family he couldn't remember.

What the hell Michael, she muttered. Why not?

He opened his arms to gesture to the house, but she was already sighing into their bedroom, gripping her head.

Left him standing by the top step, holding the banister, trying to untangle his confusion at her sudden enthusiasm for his imagination.

Each took a child for a weapon. He dressed Mara in radiator-warm pyjamas and read her *The Very Hungry Caterpillar*, and when he did the voices they came stomping down the stairs in loud boots. She bathed Louis, the tub frothing up with laughter that went splashing through the floorboards.

When the kids were asleep they ate beans on toast with a glass of wine, begrudgingly. She'd stirred in a bit of blue cheese to make them feel more middle class. Michael smiled to himself, remembering his dad calling his mum *hoity-toity* for eating a burger with a knife and fork (*But I can't fit the bun in my mouth*). Esme didn't ask why he was smiling. He didn't tell her. Between bites they stared at their phones. Michael tried very hard not to imagine the legs of her chair. Finished without a word.

Don't you think it would be insane not to?

She smiled awkwardly at the squirmed-out word, her wariness in suggesting he was insane implying that she might actually think he was insane. She plunged her wrists into the sink. The word hung unhealthily in the atmosphere.

You said not to interfere with things, he protested.

Yeah. But this wouldn't be interfering so much as, er, parrying. Think of it like a mental airbag.

She smiled, as if he just needed some gentle encouragement. He imagined the front of her face falling off like the panel of a steering wheel, the white pillow puffing out. *Well that'll never happen*, he thought.

Anyway, she said, people said they were dangerous . . .

She didn't quite sound like she was convincing herself.

. . . but you wouldn't dream of driving a car without one now.

Careful Michael, he put her voice on, *make sure you don't fuck anything up by accident.*

That wasn't what I said. And this is different. This is—

What? Your idea?

She held the knife a moment too long, let it slide on to the drying rack. They'd been here before, arguing in the kitchen – full of doors and drawers to slam, full of loud and resentful instruments. He imagined her coming at him, slashing. Cleavers. Vegetable peelers. Butter knives. Forks. (He gave the cutlery draw a quick glance – the forks had gone. She would be so quietly exasperated with him when she found out. Or not.)

How could you not want to?

Because.

Because what?

Because it feels like things are finally getting back to normal, he wanted to say. Only last night he'd brought a brick to bed.

Because I'd rather not be able to do it all, thanks.

She rolled her eyes.

If you want rid, why don't you just imagine yourself getting hit on the head by a golf ball?

He straight-batted her facetiousness. (But it was true: he'd spent embarrassing hours in the shed, repeating the exercise with a box of nails to test for vanishing skills . . . viewing himself getting golf-balled in the third person, which couldn't have been right, because he couldn't be spectator and spectacle simultaneously . . . taking the hit in the first person; equally unimaginable, since the white ball turned his mind black . . . Michael felt this revealed something integral about the nature of human consciousness, he just couldn't think exactly what that was.)

Michael—. If you can do it . . . ?

He felt the prod in her voice. Dried off the pan, passive-aggressively frustrating its clatter going back in the cupboard.

What if I can?

She turned to face him; caught him off-guard with a sharp look. Her hands were out-turned, full of bubbles.

Well then, you should know what it would mean.

She left him in the kitchen, not talking to himself. Placing the last of the knives in the drawer, he thought about it: sure, it would be an end to things, to fear, to worry, to anxiety, to the small, bird-sized voice in your head asking you, *What if the worst happened?* It would be a kind of ending, he thought, as he closed the plastic lock on the drawer.

And, huffing towards the living room in that light, he remembered the screaming, her screaming. He was coming back to her pain, holding the mirror from the downstairs toilet so she could see how far she was. None of them had met this person that was trying to enter the house, spattered in blood and body muck. (*They hadn't brought Louis home: he was born here!*) The midwife was charming and pretended to have things in hand, but there can be no controlled way to pass one human body through the body of another human. He must have blacked out in the toilet, or something, because it was almost too late. From then on, the faces hung on the walls smiled at each other awkwardly; the place wore the stench and dulled terror of a slaughterhouse. Until, after one long asphyxiated second, she had hold of an armful more breath in the room. *Louis*, she said soothingly, *Louis* – he was screaming! they were all so happy! – *Oh, Louis, I know*, she said, *I know. It's OK, lovely, you get used to it.*

Closing the bathroom window, she must have seen him trudging to the shed. Seen him say *Oh shit off* as he struggled with the lock on the shed. The door almost hit him in the face. The shed's shadeless bulb cast his shadow through the opening and into the garden. Then he closed the door, and his long shadow shrank in there after him.

The shed had a fungal stench. He had to sweep the crumbs of dirt from the camping chair before he could sit down comfortably and imagine the kids being hit by a car. First one. Then the other. All kinds of cars, just to be sure. Sometimes driving away without stopping. Sometimes the driver, lifting their floppy body. Phoning an ambulance. Standing there, in the headlamps, with their thoughts in their hands. Once or twice, he was driving. He imagined attaching flowers to a fence at the side of a nearby road. Their favourite teddy. Finding a different route to work.

He imagined one of them falling out of a tree (this time it was a yew): neck snapped, wings akimbo. He struggles to answer the calm questions of the voice on the other end of the emergency line. He watches Esme climb into the back of the ambulance after the stretcher.

Then he looks up to the tree and sees the other.

One day, one of them doesn't come home from their friend's house. Police officers in rubber gloves crawl through the barley fields, the holloway, across the golf course, heron-legged into the rough. He holds an arm around Esme as she sobs at a press conference. Every time he goes to the shops he has to walk past a picture of their face with a phone number underneath. Each year the police put out new photographs of them, showing how old they'd look now. And now. And now. And each birthday they add a candle to the cake. Until they stop buying a cake. The kids grow further and further apart; only one of them is a kid any more. Michael joins a football team and keeps getting sent off. Esme has an affair. Nobody says a thing.

There are many different kinds of staircases. This is one of the things he notices as his children are falling down them.

Now Louis is standing by himself in a corner of the playground, ripping little leaves from the bramble that reaches through the school fence. Mara hides in the toilet during playtime, writing things about the other kids on the cubicle wall.

A man in a diving suit with his face covered and an air tank on his back sinks into the water not far from where their baby was last seen. Everything is perfectly still, except for the midges blickering over the water. He surfaces again, shakes his head at the other officers. When they get home, *Everyone's been bitten*, one of them says. It just slips out, before they can reckon with *everyone* being reduced by one.

He imagined them asking again (*unthinkable*), sitting them down on the end of their bed, trying to find the right words: gentle and accurate. They try to find the right words: the ones with the right gaps, the right deflections. But both of them say that nothing ever happened, in so many words. But neither of them can get it out of their minds – *you bury these things* – as the case goes on (or after): the sight of him, entering court with his hand over his face, the hand that scooped the footballs after practice, as gently as you'd collect a baby's head.

He couldn't imagine anything worse.

He imagined a dog. Pink-gummed, mauling the struggle out of her. It gets bored, sits in the corner of the room until the police arrive and take it outside to the garden. Her body on the kitchen floor doesn't flinch at the sound of the gunshot. They appear in the newspapers in a story about a campaign in favour of harsher penalties for keeping dangerous breeds. *It's how you raise them*, said the woman on the vox pop. He tried to get right the look of them all: tosa, argentino, pit bull terrier . . .

Brushing his teeth at bedtime, the first thing they notice is the blood in the sink. They read lots of stories because it keeps him still and he is incredibly brave. He is incredibly brave as his hair falls out. He is braver than they can be when the footballers come to visit. He smiles and asks for autographs. They name a fund after him and shake buckets outside the match. People see his picture on the internet and comment about how incredibly brave he is. But his parents think that he isn't brave, he's naïve. He's incredibly naïve. When you are his age, a dull afternoon on a plastic chair is interminable – he has no idea how much time he is set to lose. At the match, on the minute that marked his age, the home crowd light up their phones and chant his name; the away crowd join in, but then cheer mutedly when their side take an early lead. The coffin is only long enough to be borne by two sets of shoulders. As everyone returns to their cars, wiping their noses on an April day, they all say how incredibly brave his little sister is, so brave. And his parents – so brave – seeing the earth they'd pay for fill such a small hole. They keep some of his clothes in the mothballed bottom drawer, fresh and ironed, as though they weren't sinking out of fashion.

He imagined how unlucky they'd feel when, a few years later, the same thing happened to her.

His face on the front of the newspaper looks so different to his face in the morgue. The other kid's face so different to the face in court. People from TV keep getting in touch about pieces on gangs and knife crime; they don't want to think about anyone, anything, touching him. Every morning, they try to lift themselves again and the word 'murder' clings to them, their pasts, their futures, like oil on feather. It might not always be graceful, but they keep him moving in their minds; away from the worst of it, carrying him as far as their lives.

He imagined it turned out to be the microwave that was faulty – she had warned him about it, repeatedly. The acrid smell of burnt fabric, melted plastic as the grey morning gave up the dew on the grass out the front, the hose-damp pavement and the two small bags they carried them out in. Next time it would be the fridge. The time after that, the TV.

First it was just nails – barely perceptible. *Scratched it on a bush.* Then the hook on a nail file. Kitchen scissors. A knife. In the house. Miles away behind the bedroom door. *What's she doing in there?* Just the faint light of the screen shining through the gap beneath the door, the far horizon of the lighthouse.

This train seems to take forever. Its headlamps spool more and more shadow from their boy. Then the train shrieks. There is a small, fleshy thud. Luminous jackets emerge to gather the evidence. People are late. But eventually the line is clear. Carriages breeze by.

A ball rolls over the sidings and between the lines. Any minute his sister will step on to the track.

He trailed the smell of damp wood and spiders in with him. Esme pretended to be half-asleep, hugged him, mumbling. He was cold. They'd have to get a heater for the shed.

Sleepily, they tangled: an arm under one neck, another arm over a shoulder, one arm across a waist and a leg knotted inside another leg – so, drifting off, Michael felt a hand feeling a head and wasn't sure if it was his hand or her hand. They hadn't slept so close since the accident.

Once, in the single bed at his parents' house, she'd fallen asleep with his arm under her head and he didn't dare wake her; so he left it to tingle, ache and then deaden: a ghost's arm, touching the world without feeling a thing. He'd have been about twenty-one, twenty-two, and his fifteen-year-old self was amazed that he managed to get a woman like her into his bedroom.

For the only time he could remember, he kissed her. She barely moved.

On either side of the bed, their phones waited for them blankly. He wouldn't sleep tonight – his head loud with police lights, landing alarms. Over the noise of sirens he could remember them eating together, walking together, drinking together. If he could stay awake long enough, he thought, he might remember the emergency of them falling in love.

Upstairs, under their duvet, with the world breathing on their window: it all felt so safe. He didn't expect to sleep. Eventually, night would ebb and there'd be the left-behind shadows of things, straggled around. But now, on the other side of the glass, the night wood held a finger to its lips – its slow, thick darkness levelled with the dark beneath their car, the dark under the stairs, the dark beneath their beds, poured into their drawers' dark, the dark in their wardrobes, the dark in their mouths – how a tide consumes crab pools, gullies, sewers, coming in to claim its world. He stared into it. Nothing moved.

18

What shall we do today?

The aggravation had gone from her throat, as though a good night's sleep had made her younger – her voice lighter, emptier. Not the usual cave-damp, calcite sleep, its dark encroachments; the half-sleep of feeling the way along the walls for a piss. He remembered them sitting up in bed (was it the first time they'd slept together?) and Esme asking, *What shall we do today?* as though she'd decided that this was them, now: they spent their days together.

Haven't you got work?

She grinned, as if to say *just this once*, without knowing exactly how to justify her new insouciance.

They drove out to a picnic spot that Esme knew. Copper water gurgled through the hills and the kids' feet were amphibious creatures, discovering the moss-fuzzed stones, the veils of silt. Louis pioneered across the river; it was less treacherous than he'd hoped, and you couldn't see all the way home from the top, but it was almost cloud-high, afloat on the crest of sheep shit and grass – but Daddy was down there waving and smiling, small and far; he only had to put his hand out to disappear Daddy completely. Louis, dazed into the world, as though he'd never been born. Mara kept petting the river with fat slaps, soaking Esme, who'd waded out with her, one hand bunching up her skirt, the other hand holding her daughter's. Self-consciously, Michael photographed everything, filmed everything (Esme laughed at him to stop embarrassing them), stared at everything; he'd lost so much of his children's lives and here they were, still becoming themselves constantly as the sun found another glint of water and another and the clouds turned into other clouds. To the coach-trip pensioners, shielding their eyes from the sun, they must have looked like their younger days – the backward dream of themselves with a family and future. There was more sky than Michael had seen for ages: it was overwhelming. And with the kids in their own worlds, he smiled at Esme, who smiled back as though she was thinking the exact same thing. As the smile wore itself out, he weighed it up: are we pretending to be a normal couple for them, or are we pretending we are a normal couple for us?

But that any of this could vanish only made the performance of hills and sky and sunlight feel more incredible on the small stage of his family.

So the world outside came to feel like a hospital: he was dazed, ecstatic, terrified and only faintly awake, the cool morphine of the outdoor light hazing its way into him. Sitting on the grassy bank, he felt a lightness, and at the same time as though he was this stone weight that sagged the canvas of the hills towards this depression where his kids played in the water and the undulating stream played with the light on his wife's skin. He remembered being two feet out to sea somewhere with Esme, chasing her back up the beach – back when they were still young enough to kick water at each other and old enough for it to be serious: one of those fluidities that somehow becomes a moment. There must have been all kinds like it; he had no idea why this one reinvented itself in his head. *It's all so accidental*, he thought, taking himself seriously, *being a person*. He'd wanted to bring it up, but didn't know how without sounding nostalgic or French. He rubbed the 'ancient treasure' pebble Mara had doled out to him. She had a bucket full of them, lifted up from the stream for Mummy's museum. He smiled, thinking of people inclining to read the note beneath the case: 'Mara's stones'.

On the drive back, Esme caught him yawning.

Almost home, she said.

Remember when you soaked me at the beach? he splurted.

Err—

We went for a paddle and you kicked water all over me? So I chased you down the beach? Years ago? You were wearing a white dress?

Are all of your cherished memories about other women?

The look she gave him only made him want to prove the point.

Uh? It was you. Can't you remember? It was grey, muggy. We were at the beach.

She had this dismissive breath instead of a laugh. It sounded like picking stitches. He gave in. Wiped the forehead grease on the window with the sleeve of his jacket. It spread.

Hey, she said, tapping his thigh, could you make gnocchignese for dinner tomorrow?

Make what?

But the knot in his eyebrows undid; he could feel the rich warmth of it, the soft mounds of gnocchi surrounded by Bolognese, under a snowfall of Parmesan; he'd made it for her years ago, semi-improvised from leftovers, when it was raining and the bus was wheezing by and she was wading into the lurgy he'd just shaken off – and now it was their dish, the one they ate sick, or celebrating, or because it was Tuesday and seeing the kids scooping it into their daft tomato grins was enough to get them to Wednesday.

Sure, said Michael, trying to suppress the smile a little, feeling as though Esme had discovered him for himself.

When they got home, Louis and Mara were still dead to the world. Lifting the jackpot of kids from the car, sand poured from their untied shoes, their drooping sleeves, smuggling time. The neighbours smiled, on their way to the pub; the houses around them glowing into the dusk. It was all so safe – the clouds plumped over their heads like a pillow. Nothing bad could come.

I'll clean the car tomorrow, he volunteered.

Yeah, she said as she stepped into the house with a puzzled look on her face, it stinks of dog, doesn't it?

17

Coma patients are rated on the Glasgow Scale. Michael fell as low as three. Any lower than three and they stoke the fire at the crematorium. Fifteen is the highest grade: at fifteen your eyes are open; you know who, where and when you are. Fifteen is *Congratulations, you're not in a coma!* It felt unfair to think of all the idiots he'd met; they'd all get full marks. Because now he felt far past fifteen. All his life he'd sensed that there was something just beyond his thoughts, something important, something he should be able to articulate – the slim shadow of a thought, creeping between the folded shadows of his thoughts. Some word, some gesture.

Now he'd found a means to shape it properly. Only slowly, at first, and in the odd thing: a brick, a football, a Coke can. He could sense the nothing of them, feel it. Then, piece by piece, in everything: how tenuous it all was. How the world that seemed so robust – knotted with people and brambles, the insects stitching the air together, the weeds growing out from brick walls – it was all an articulation of nothing. All so uncertain, except in its endings. That the backward certainty of an end guaranteed the astonishing luck of a beginning. That was what he could feel: all things on the edge of their fall. How everything was trying to replace itself, terrified and ecstatic, goaded on by its own nothing. How loudly it was all underscored by silence. How even the tiniest, shivering leaves are mortgaged so hugely against themselves. Feeling the nothing of everything, knowing he could erase it all with so little as a thought, the world felt more real to him than ever. The way a great white shark must feel: with one kick, the whole ocean shivers.

For days now, it was exhilarating. His brain thundered with things. With the nothing of things. The half-screwed handle of the shed door, its tarnished brass effect, seemed miraculous. The bucket, the cobwebs, the mouldy gloves: miraculous.

Louis was alive!

Mara was alive!

Esme was alive!

He was alive!

But there, like a monitor's pulse, was always this thought . . . In the morning, he counted them. Louis. Mara. Esme. Him. He counted the houses. He counted the trees. Never had he made anyone disappear. Not since Max, never. Never even a bit of them – he was sure, because he'd concentrated.

First thing, though, when he woke: Louis. Mara. Esme. Him.

★

There was the sun again, against all the odds, behind the clouds. And already the kids were down in the garden, playing with the bees, inventing spring. And didn't it sound like the birds were singing for their lives?

16

Nice to see you back, said everyone.

Work took Michael by surprise, with its real plants and real people. Lucia (egg-sandwich woman?) had set an out-of-office response – 'I'm in a coma. If it's urgent, wake me up. Michael' – that had apparently caused a ruckus in the staff kitchen. At his back-to-work meeting, the boss squirmed in her ergonomic chair as though he was unsackable now (he'd heard the word *redundancy* surging like teenage acne through office chatter). Their gentleness worried him, everyone treating him as though a knock to the head was infectious. He supposed they'd all squeezed together in a store cupboard or toilet cubicle, discussed his injuries and decided on how they'd deal with him. They knew something and they weren't letting on.

It turned out that the only thing insurance-claims handling required was an eye for mendacity and the ability to admit when things were too complicated – qualities Michael prized. But the first few times the phone rang he pretended he couldn't hear it. Then he imagined it ringing, and now the phone in his head wouldn't stop.

Hello? he'd answer it in his mind; they always had the wrong number. The office was half-populated, its chairs empty in a way that made 'working from home' seem like a dictatorship euphemism. There was the odd person he thought he recognised from school – the sweaty lip, the jar head, the dolphin laugh – as though they'd all been held back in some elaborate remedial class. Staring at the spreadsheet, he knew he was making a mistake somewhere along the line, but had no idea where.

Low-level chatter, waiting to be kicked out, people spooking about the place: he'd felt this edginess before . . . those damp weekends in seaside arcades, Luc's fake 20ps insisting they play that faded Pac-Man, even though there were driving and zombie-shooting games; Pac-Man's insatiable lack, his narrow corridors, his approaching ghosts – the tension headache would set in, sea-fog thick, his Sundays a pain behind the eyes. He felt its approach.

The familiarity of it seeped into him, just as the office smell infects your clothes. This had been every day; and one day, without warning, he'd been uprooted from it all, so now what was he doing back? (The thought of his mum trying to convince Uncle Mike not to move to the other side of the world; his uncle pulling her monstera out of the pot, letting soil fall all over her living-room floor and giggling, *We're not plants!* and against all her manners, his mum having to laugh, too, even though she was stung by him moving away, the way it passed judgement on her narrow life, and sulked – because even though she had a mum's responsibilities now, she was still his Big Sister. More and more these memories spreading into the dark, he felt as though he was getting a grip of himself.) Michael looked at the plant nearby and smiled, imagining it prising itself from the pot, draping its roots over a leafy arm like a bridal train, its flowery head checking left, then right, before it made a dash for the door.

And coughed, as though he was choking and not laughing at a plant, since they were about to ask.

At lunch, he escaped with his sandwiches to the woods. There were some tents by the underpass, blankets and sun-bleached cans, but no sign of anyone around. It didn't take far into the woods for the sound of the road to soften into the anxiousness of leaves. Perched on the trunk of a fallen tree, he nibbled at the ham and cheese sandwich he'd bought from the petrol station. He almost didn't go back into the office. Imagined his colleagues duct-taping him in the meeting room while they argued over whether to get him committed or to kill him and hide the body in the pond with the shopping trolleys, the dead bottles. Everyone here was so nice to each other's faces that their faces had become out-of-office responses.

But he was already at his desk when he resolved not to return. Idiotically, he'd expected to discover his real self in this office, as though the lumbar support chair had some revelatory quality: the Turin Shroud of office furniture. As soon as he accepted that this wasn't him, not really – that it was him pretending to be him, the way Lucia was pretending to be Lucia; Mark, Mark; Jude, Jude, etc., that none of them were properly here, and that i.e. work Jude was only a performance of Judeness, that she wasn't truly that woman who spun ninety-degrees on her chair to answer the phone, *Hello Jude Armstrong?* as if her doppelgänger were on the line – that really, it was a chimera designed to protect their real selves from work, from offices, from colleagues, from management, from money – then he decided he might actually quite like work. He felt like standing on his desk and giving a broad-grinned speech, *I'm back and this is work!*

Then he thought of the slow, sarcastic applause that would follow his big discovery about work, which everyone else had known all along. (He didn't worry that the real Michael might be the Michael pretending to be himself at work. Not then, anyway.)

The afternoon was spent deleting emails while he imagined the cancers that could prise him cell from cell. Colon, liver, lung, throat, stomach, intestine, brain, breast. (Was there such a thing as toe cancer? He imagined himself dying of it – one obnoxious onion of a toe.) Coat Michael (so called on account of the rumour he never wore a coat) came over from the Property team to joke about comas being a nominative affliction. John (was it John?) kept going on about his *Not-the-littlest's* birthday party (*macaron castle! pony-riding! famous magician! limousine to the leisure centre!*) as though he was arranging an oligarch's summit on climate change. Michael pictured himself wearing a winter scarf to Mara's summer birthday, hiding the tumour growing from his neck in case it put the kids off their cupcakes. He'd tried imagining them as 'not millionaires', so why they were still not millionaires confounded him. But then money always did. (At least the letters from the bank had stopped appearing since he pictured them being forced through the door.) If the best he could do for his kids was to imagine them washed up on a beach, bloated and straggled in a life jacket stuffed with newspaper and plastic bottles, then that was the best he could do. And when someone said,

You don't let them play out by the road, do you?

he started to giggle – tried to deflect it with a cough, seal his hand over it, but the laughter wouldn't stop.

Sorry, he said. Pretending he was choking on something. They'd be fine! Esme, the kids! Here he was, only pretending to work as an insurance-claims handler by working as an insurance-claims handler. The rest of the office went home to themselves: to children, to TV, dog walks, five-a-side, BDSM, sudoku – he went home to his shed to imagine bullet wounds, substation explosions, falling trees. Nothing could touch them! They'd be completely fine!

At hometime, he waved at his new/old colleagues, getting into their cars which could be crushed by trucks or spin wildly off a verge and into a ditch and explode, or heading for their trains which might derail into the station or be hijacked by terrorists, or walking along the shady lanes, hedged with attackers and angry dogs.

At hometime, he went home.

15

Sometimes life comes easy, as it does for trees or butterflies or cats. You barely notice yourself having to try and be human. It was as if Esme didn't mind in the slightest the cold blast in the still-dark morning, standing on the platform with her flask of coffee steaming red around her nostrils. The first light would be beginning to pool in the depressions in the burnt fields, and between emails she'd be composing her daily five 'events' (his limit, with one extra usually snuck in), weighing up school-trip bus crashes and teenage pregnancies. From there on the puzzle of her skeleton fell into place – Janice asked her if she'd taken up mindful yoga or Buddhism, Alisha commented on how radiant her skin was looking and wondered if she'd given up gluten, and those half-known people about the museum would try to figure out, as she smiled past them, whether they recognised her or not.

With everything so secure, she could get back to the bits of herself that trailed off years ago – that work she'd promised herself on gods and oracles in cultures in decline – only with all the knowledge of catastrophe that having kids brings. Even during her lunch, which she ate outside in the square with the pigeons and the tourists and the homeless encampment in the bushes, her cravings to check her phone to see if the nursery or the school had called fell away. Because in the nursery Mara was safe in a world of her own, painting pictures and inventing games as though the whole planet was just odds and ends stacked around, waiting to be built. The other kids flocked behind her because it seemed that with her anything could happen, even if a little way up the road in primary school nothing happened to Louis: no cuts, no grazes, no bad words, no falls, no humiliations. All day, clouds grazed across his face and aeroplanes drew chalk lines where they floated on the surface of the window.

Michael didn't mind being cramped back into emails and phone calls and spreadsheets and the ongoing clash of idealism versus realpolitik over the milk in the staff kitchen. Or the chatter of hand-arm vibration claims, road-traffic accidents, NIHL, RSI, mesothelioma, carpal tunnel syndrome, cancers, silicosis and dermatitis. His body had automated disaster. Everyone agreed about how well he'd rebounded. Trish, who was going to be a political cartoonist before she'd grown up, even drew a little sketch of her walking past Michael, laid out on the floor by the golf ball, with a speech bubble coming from her mouth: *You lucky bastard*. He kept it on his desk. And all because he was unlucky enough to be knocked to the floor and land in a coma, he got to fall for Esme again – to find himself needing to make her laugh, to touch her whenever he could, to delve into her past even though she'd already told him everything, so that an evening of the sofa and chocolate digestives felt like dusk cocktails on the Riviera. He got to go home to a new world. Pulling up with the kids in the back seats to his house, which wasn't going to set on fire, or crumble in an earthquake, or be crashed into by a plane or a helicopter, infested by wasps, ants, cockroaches, snakes, bears, smashed to pieces by a meteorite, or even give them all respiratory diseases from damp, he sometimes thought to himself: *You lucky bastard.*

14

But there's only so long you can sit in the shed imagining things from existence. There's the school run. The supermarket. Evenings at the leisure centre. *Isn't this what you wanted?* said Esme. *Things back to normal?* And they were! Except the homeostasis of eating the kids' food and sofa-basking wasn't quite what she had in mind. Maybe she had a point: they could play *Michael & Esme* impeccably at home – and sure, it was good fun – but what's the point in all those rehearsals unless you also get to play *Esme & Michael* in public? People would be happy to see them *thriving* (was this his mum's word?) again – as though the social body needs to see successful examples of coupledom, otherwise its whole ecosystem would fracture into reckless polyamory. Or we'd drift apart to live as hermits in cars. He understood it intuitively, though: part of being a couple is showing off, its confidential body language of touch and glance and smile that conveys an enormous and untellable secret – (us!). Plus, there's a certain glee that comes with knowing your secret is more enormous than most.

★

So a month after first sitting up in bed to eat solid food, Michael was lounging in a restaurant booth, ordering something with celeriac purée, waiting to be introduced to his oldest friend, Lucas. Lucas, who was *so supportive* during the coma and insisted on taking them out for dinner, *whenever you're ready*. He was running late and had messaged Esme to order for him. So they waited. Nodding at each other. Smiling. Saying little.

Luc had requested they eat somewhere further around the city's circumference. Esme drove over, while they sang along to songs he could sort of half-remember the words to, imagining the car veering across the lanes, flipping over into a ditch, bursting into flames, being crushed by trucks, etc. They arrived safely.

It was one of those inns with an addendum of a restaurant, the kind with a doorway plaque bragging about a nearby medieval battle, battle-faced regulars wearing down the barstools. The restaurant was candle-lit and cramped with noise, all chatter and chewing under roofbeams stitched to the old inn's beams and artificially aged. The kind of place where endings felt furthest away.

His oldest friend didn't so much arrive as appear, perfectly attired like a TV host, as though the world had panned to him.

Luc! said Esme.

Hey! Look at you! he pointed at Michael. Breathing all by your fucking self!

Michael nodded, idiotically, as though he was proud of his respiratory skills. Esme looked up in glee as Luc titled an avuncular head and rested his hand on the air at bed height.

Last time I saw you, you were only this high.

Everybody laughed. He didn't not recognise this Lucas – for some reason, Michael had expected a twelve-year-old boy to walk through the door, even though he'd been responding to a grown man's text messages for the last few weeks post-coma. If his face was unfamiliar, his presence was recognisable. He had the grace and competency of someone who was actually human, rather than just giving it a go. The way he strode through everything made Michael feel as though he was still dangling one foot from the edge of his hospital bed, waiting for the floor to rise up and meet it. He found himself wanting to disappear a wine glass or the barman's beard to impress him, if only that didn't have the grubbiness of a birthday-party clown.

Nothing he could think to say seemed sensible, or intelligent, or interesting, or witty, or coherent enough. Which was fine, because Esme and Luc could talk and laugh. And he could just stare at his knife and fork until the food arrived: the pair tucked up in a napkin, sleeping alongside each other like husband and wife. (Michael was disorientated into a memory of standing to give a speech, speechless. It was their wedding. *Esme*, he paused. Then by accident said, *thanks for coming*. Everybody laughed. He pretended, as with so many other things in his life, that it was deliberate.)

So, tell me all about it, Lucas eventually asked between mouthfuls of tenderloin, as though Michael had been on holiday to St Lucia.

Erm, he said.

He'd been emailing Michael's work account while he was in hospital (*Dear Sleeping Beauty, What's new?*) with links to articles about people who never woke from their comas. He couldn't tell if this meant that his friend had been optimistic he'd wake up and find it funny, or was anxious that he wouldn't and had resorted to superstition.

Apparently I was out for a walk when I got hit on the head by a golf ball.

I know! And also: did you fuck, Luc laughed. Nobody gets hit on the head by a golf ball. It's like getting struck by lightning flying a kite. Or falling down a manhole eating a sandwich.

I did. It was in the paper and everything.

Ha! yeah . . . Emse, he said with a knowing smile at Michael's wife.

He was about to enquire about this private joke, but Luc hurried on into something else inexplicable.

La Guerre du Golfe n'a pas eu lieu. Anyway, he said, serves you both right for moving back to that fucking timewarp and planting yourselves next to a golf course. Butterflies playing caterpillars.

Esme rolled her eyes, but not as though she meant it.

OK – fine, it's safe-ish out there, nostalgic. Bucolic. Whatever. But can't you remember the utter fucking tedium of our childhood?

He jostled Michael's shoulder.

Yeah, he said while googling 'bucolic' on his phone under the table.

It was difficult to tell from the way he moved, the way he spoke, but there was a shadow of resemblance to the best mate who'd encouraged him to lob a cow pat at the postman while singing the theme tune from a kids' programme. Maybe not – this suit would never fit that boy.

Still, he reasoned, we don't so much grow into our clothes as out of ourselves.

You could hear the shitting grass grow. It was insufferable.

It's nice! said Esme. Quiet. Trees. Clean air. Cleaner.

Luc let slip a fat, wry laugh.

The farmers are poisoning you like fucking badgers, he said.

Esme looked into Luc's eyes as though they'd been through this so many times they could let it play out in their minds. Luc grinned, his left arm resting on the back of Esme's chair.

Seriously! This is a miracle! Fucking, Mr Potato Head here, the fucking nineteenth hole, was hit by a golf ball – almost fucking died – but didn't! – and you don't look at the world and think: here, still? He's been to the fucking underworld!

It was a coma, not a katabasis.

Esme, Luc said as he placed his right hand on hers. We don't all share your medical knowledge.

Ancient Greek, she said with an inscrutable smile, *katabasis*: go down.

Somehow, in one movement, Luc managed to laugh knowingly at Esme and order another bottle of wine from a passing waitress, without ever making it seem as though he was laughing at the waitress or ordering the bottle of wine from Esme. It was impressive (to Michael, at least, who would have fucked it up and spent the rest of the night grinning apologetically at the waitress). Still, he felt as though he'd been dragged to a crap play that had no point and would get gushing reviews in the broadsheets.

It'll go down nicely, Luc added – who knew he shouldn't have, but in the end couldn't resist, because somewhere he must have known Esme would laugh as though it was actually funny.

Lucas kept pointing his fork at Esme whenever she said something, as though he was trying to pin her down. This wasn't the Esme that Michael had met in the hospital. The way she laughed, she seemed younger; he remembered her in a dump of a student house – they were housemates, her and Luc, weren't they? – doing a headstand on the couch, singing Diana Ross's 'Upside Down'. Is that how he'd met her, through Luc? Through Luc he was meeting her again. She was eating her aubergine with one hand, prodding and squeezing Luc with the other, explaining something about *persistent vegetative state* and asking people to *imagine they're playing tennis*. At one point she tapped Michael on the arm – he could join in any minute – then glanced back at his silence with a look as though she expected someone else to be sitting there. He didn't say a word.

The waitress kept drifting past to see if they'd finished yet. She had the face of someone who'd been tricked by a fairy-tale witch, gaining eternal youth at the cost of serving food in a succession of mid-scale restaurants until the end of the world. He imagined Mara trapped and miserable, serving wet spaghetti. And considered imagining the waitress stuck here forever – wondered if that was too presumptuous, too interfering, misguided . . . Realised he was smiling at her, sympathetically and out of context. The look she returned showed how creepy he seemed.

★

His wife and best friend were still grappling over Michael: his near-death, his near-life. He felt as though he was a teenager, taken out for dinner on his birthday by his divorced parents, who may or may not have been reconsidering things.

You're getting better, aren't you?

Esme touched his hand, waking him back up to the conversation.

It was so cute . . . Mara said to me the other day, Daddy's more Daddy now, isn't he.

You go on like I'm some sad case – I'm fine.

Course, she said, with her hand in his hair, running her thumb across the mark on his temple. Just a little knock.

But he flinched from her, glowered. Esme bent her head towards her plate, eating moodily. Luc arched his eyebrows indecipherably, ran his fingers through his hair again, as though he was trying to draw attention to what was, in all fairness, excellent hair; against all reason, Michael felt as though he was being goaded to vanish it.

They ate in silence, before Luc rescued the mood –

Guess who I saw the other day? You remember Kaz?! – distracting their sullen quietude into a story about someone from uni who always posted photos of a negative space tattoo of her (dead) fiancé's face on her shoulder (so *He'd always be there, watching over me*) – which Luc thought was hilarious, Esme not quite so much. They joked with their mouths full.

And Michael stared at Luc; something of him recalled his uncle. He worked in finance, too, only in a different time zone. He could see the appeal – betting on the future, of being a kind of oracle. One spectacular success to cover the countless losses. They both had that sense of being everywhere and nowhere at once, citizens of the world. You couldn't be like them and live where he and Esme lived – it wasn't one of those posh commuter towns. It was mostly bordered with barbed wire and corrugated-steel barns, slip roads and concrete manufacturers. Even though you only had to throw a stone over the motorway to hit a farmer, the barnheads mostly kept to themselves; town kids only went to their houses to buy puppies. He'd been, hadn't he? The barn swayed with cows. The musty stench of them was so strong it had formed a mist, a kind of spook inhabiting the place. Apparently they all had names, the cows, but it didn't seem fair to speak them in front of the cows in case they got attached. Another thing they'd lose. Had he asked what they do with the cows? That didn't seem like him. But he could hear this kid's voice telling him that they *Load them in a truck and zap them in the head. For being cows.*

Branded. Michael chewed, thinking about their last bit of cud, whether they'd remember being dragged by the heel from their mother's lickings, the walks up the lane, huddling in the steaming barn, cool grass on hot days, or whether they really had anything to be forgotten by the blast of voltage in their forehead, before being shoved off for butchering into cuts and laid as gently as a dreaming head on to the searing pan.

Has everyone finished?

The waitress intervened.

No, I've—

But when Luc looked down to his plate, it was empty, except for a nub of carrot. Esme glared at the plate.

Michael offered a faint smile to his friend, a muted *Tada!*, who had no idea a trick had taken place. For the first time tonight, Luc looked less than in command of the situation, gawping at the plate, chewing his words. In no time at all, everything was cleared up.

Even the trees waved goodbye to Luc on his way for the train, the sky a broad and goldening smile and the motorway (just over the hill) pretending to be the sea. Walking across the car-park gravel, Esme turned to Michael and glowered, sighed.

You couldn't have at least pretended to be friendly? she said.

Uh?

It's bad enough with Mara – but *you*, sulking, playing up. Fine, I know it's been hard, but he was so kind and attentive while you were in the coma.

I'll bet he was, thought Michael, not brave enough to goad her. So he looked perplexed by her instead.

You know he sat there and read to you. And I remember thinking, if anyone's voice will reach him down there, it'll be Luc's.

I was friendly, wasn't I? said Michael, thinking *I barely know the man*.

She ignored him.

★

It was one of those evenings when the birds seem to have discovered the sun's largesse and stretch themselves across the sky, or sit in the near trees, tangling up in song. One of those evenings when winter and absence and retreat seem impossible. Michael glanced over his shoulder towards the white pub, the cellar door half-open to the dark. Esme stopped walking.

You didn't even say *thanks* when he paid for dinner, she continued.

I did!

Michael groaned.

I'm sorry if I'm not smart enough to join in. That I don't have opinions about historical figures or plays. Next time, why don't you set me some homework beforehand. I'll do some flashcards.

Fucking hell, Michael. You're like a teenage boy.

I thought we had a laugh, me and you – but you're just patronising me, aren't you? Poorly, stupid Michael.

She laughed, incredulous.

Right, she said.

A couple waddled past towards the restaurant, trying not to look at them, the meld of their loud perfumes sealing them in their own weather. Michael was still trying to untwist the knot of his face when Esme began to walk away.

Esme!

She turned, but he didn't know what came next. Lingered there, in the clammy, creamy gush from the kitchen ventilators, feeling completely misplaced. Hungry swifts were clearing the air. The pub cat had stalked along the fence, as though it might pull a bird from the air with a sly paw – then it caught sight of Michael and Esme standing apart from each other in the car park, saw itself being seen, and fell from the fence. Its claws scrabbled for a ledge, until it gave up and let itself drop into the bush. Michael wanted to laugh. That's where he wanted to be – Esme leaning her head on him, the pair of them laughing together at the daft cat, momentarily forgetting its catness.

Neither of them did.

Esme rolled her eyes, shook her head, sighed: the holy trinity of disdain. The kids needed picking up. The swifts' shadows were landing in the shadows of the trees. It was too late for all of this.

He stalked her towards the car. And the thought of her, on the phone to her sister, *I just feel a bit trapped and bored, you know? Stifled . . . I dunno. I keep thinking about what I could be doing* – he didn't realise what he'd done. Not even when she halted, half into the car, as though she'd lost something. He just presumed that it had hit her: no matter how much fun they had together, she'd married below herself, she'd settled. That it was bad enough pre-coma, with the noise of redundancy and arrears, but now this. Him. The silence of it.

Esme started the engine.

Come on, then.

He must have looked as if he'd had a lobotomy, staring at the car.

Get in – your mum can only cope with the kids so long.

His face on the window, annoyed at itself. At the prospect of being enclosed in there, pretending to be heading in the same direction.

Aren't you coming? Michael?

Who the hell does she think she is?

Birds goaded him on. The whole way to the station he kicked stones and dandelions, replaying the argument, muttering to himself about how she was trying to get him sectioned. Or at least levering him out of things. Eventually they'd divorce and he'd spend alternate weekends taking the kids for sad trips to McDonald's and the cinema, his phone blasting the dark, checking his acca on the three o'clock kick-offs.

The nearest station was a two-platform plank of grey and weather – too far from the city centre to qualify for a waiting room or a coat of paint, too near to receive trains with empty seats. There was a third track, slowly being consumed by weeds on a long march towards the city.

Michael sank his neck into his shoulders against niggling gusts. Their lager aftertaste of track and wire and rusty water, and the faint stench of post-industrial plants at the edge of things. Glaring at the screen, its list of stations scrolling by, the thought of sitting in a pub approached. It must have been Christmas, not long after he'd started seeing Esme, because he and Luc were back home (yes! that was Luc – he felt sure of him now, the hair, the confidence . . .) in the pub in town, trying to avoid the dickheads from school who spent every other night *down the Oak*. He remembered him, between sips: *So, what's the deal with you and Es?* And Michael probably shrugged – he usually did – and said something like, *Out of my depth, aren't I?* (When the deal was they'd sleep together, and he'd tell her everything he could about his childhood, because she told him absolutely nothing about hers, no matter how much he asked. So she'd be lying there on his chest, listening to him talk about the weird man who collected glasses at the Royal Oak, with his lock-up full of car magazines and no car; about him and Luc playing football with a Malaysian kid who lived with the foster family on Offa St and said he was in a secret Premier League Academy and definitely didn't work in the WHSmith; getting chased by farmers who shouted at Luc, *Wait till your dad hears, you little prick!*) And Luc asked him, *You serious, then?* Michael rotated his pint on the mat, stared at the paler ring stains on the table – couldn't remember saying a thing.

He'd squirmed his way on to the first train, nabbing a seat and turning to the window before the moral culpability of seeing someone hobbling or pregnant in the aisle could be his. Behind him, a man talked down the phone about how the *invoices were all wrong – if we have to let them go under, we'll have to let them go under.* Michael had to dig his fingers into his palm to stop himself imagining some vital part of him.

The train chuntered along on his grievances. She had a way of making him feel like an attempt at a person, like one of Mara's drawings of him. All he could manage to vengefully imagine was that Esme would be able to turn the windscreen wipers off. It was barely even a practical joke. *The man with the devastating imagination*, he pictured her saying when she found out it was his fault they were stuck squealing back and forth, *has no such thing*.

When she lived in the flatshare by the station with Lucas and Impossible Hannah (who once confused her kidneys with her appendix and said she didn't have any), he spent an entire afternoon jailed in their kitchen, stuffing a brace of chicken breasts with home-made pesto in an attempt to convince her that he was a plausible human being. Somehow, Luc slipped off into the evening with two raw breasts in his pockets, leaving a pair of tinfoil parcels in the oven: empty, except for a slice of tomato each. All the while pans simmered, he held her hostage in the living room, impressing her with the things he'd memorised about Homer, most of which turned out to be tediously misguided. The oven's alarm saved her from his conversation. After a few minutes of sullen clatter, Esme came into her galley kitchen to find him having a breakdown over two plates of boiled potatoes and broccoli. For the first time that night she laughed genuinely, trying to pull a sympathetic face, laughing until she needed the wall to stop her from trembling on to the floor.

Then they ordered pizza and screwed.

Looking out through his reflection on the train window, the city's edgelands had conceded gaps to clumps of grass and thuggish brambles; behind the palisade fences and barbed wire, brown scabs of land grew stones and old car parts. This was the kingdom of his dad's stories: Jonny Cochran and the dartboard, the infamous potato heist and Maggie Clay's three-legged champion greyhound. Everywhere looked as if it smelled of petrol and rotten wood, as though there'd been a shelling campaign while he was asleep. People, grazing past the shuttered pubs to the newsagents, the betting shops, seemed dazed and leftover, the way sheep do.

He thought about telling the kids his stories, when they were older, then realised: he had no future. Or at least, his present had no future. He couldn't anticipate anything, couldn't look forward to anything, without the danger of destroying it. He'd known it ever since he stood in the garden with no brick in his hand; but now, being dragged backwards past the kebab shops, the fenced-in schools, and now graffitied industrial estates giving way to sodden allotments, and now fields in a sulk, that lone tree, having to take whatever comes, he felt it. Narrowing their futures, most things he could stop; whatever happened to him, though, would come from nowhere.

The voice behind banged Michael's seat, crossing his legs. He didn't turn to say anything (*You're too polite!* said Esme in his head) – just imagined the man's shoes fitting him perfectly, forever. All the while the train chuckled along the line. One end of the world disappeared out of the other end of the window.

Back from the station, for a short while Michael lurked by the tree outside his house. All the birds were shouting over each other. Every few minutes the luminous jackets digging a hole for broadband at the end of the road would look up to check he was still there; he'd pretend to be investigating for signs of ash dieback on the willow tree.

Something must have shaken, because a car alarm went off a few doors down with no sign of anyone nearby and the tree shattered into flight.

Lucky fuckers, he said, watching the birds escape and wondering what it would be like to be able to take off at the first sign of trouble, skirting over the messy earth.

Eventually, he relented; crept in the front door and peered into the kitchen where Esme was dancing with Mara to songs from before either of them were born. He smiled at her nervously; she smiled back, asked how his journey was, as though nothing had happened.

Fine, he said. Do you fancy stuffed chicken for dinner? Or pizza?

Oh, I've already got dinner in the oven for the kids – I was just gonna have a bite of theirs.

He nodded; she hadn't understood. But apparently they'd already forgiven each other.

There wasn't anything to be said. Michael drifted away. All of his life he'd felt as though he'd fallen into things: marriage, insurance, parenthood, a coma. But at the foot of the stairs he hesitated.

Have you been on the train, Daddy?

Michael, leaning on the banister, smiled at his son.

What are you drawing?

Louis shrugged. He'd been at it again: sketching car crashes, plane wrecks, derailed trains – rubbing them out, never happy with them; the page imbricated with faint impressions.

They were worried about him – *Kids grow strange*, Michael had said unconvincingly to Esme, *it's probably a phase* – but he didn't know what to imagine, didn't know what this behaviour could become. The indeterminacy of the boy's glare made his dad feel as though he was fading into the cream wall, the way we obliviate the sound of our blood before it deafens us. So he stepped down the stairs and picked up his son.

Yep, he repeated as though it indicated something important, I came home on the train.

Striding into the kitchen, he bowled Louis down into the music and grabbed his dancing wife. She was hard to hold, laughing and dancing; he hadn't quite caught up. She'd always found his little flutters of gangliness endearing, smiling as they mangled into an almost rhythm.

I love you, he said into her ear.

I love you too, she said, grabbing him closer.

He leaned back a touch.

No, you don't understand. I love you. I mean, not in the way people say it. I actually love you.

Don't people normally mean it?

Yeah, yeah, but not that way. Look at you: you're like – beautiful, and smart – and you know . . .

She smiled, bit her lip. He seemed so awake: brighter, more sudden – as though all of his intangibilities had risen to the skin. She could touch him. He was here, moving through it all, moving.

It's not like when people say *I love you* because they've settled for someone, he said. Or like a kid, when they don't know any better. I actually love you. Properly.

I love you too, she smiled, lifting her hand away from her mouth.

He didn't quite believe her – felt as though she was just trying to get him to stop his awkward, sudden spill of emotion. (He remembered bringing Kirsty daffodils from the roundabout after she'd dumped him between Biology and History – standing outside her house with the uprooted flowers while the radio shouted at him from her bedroom window and her nan came out with an Orange Club biscuit: part-sympathy, part-bribe. But this wasn't that.)

But, you're – I mean. It's nice to have me around and stuff, but –

Michael, I love you!

Unsure of herself, Mara had stopped dancing to glare at her incomprehensible parents. They smiled at her. Not just from selfishness or instinct or responsibility: Michael felt he had something worth protecting, something that proved his life, all of their lives, against nothing. Esme spun him around laughing, so they were facing the opposite way. Holding his wife, he imagined planes coming down to land through the roof, the floor becoming a hole in the ground, explosions breaking through the wall. *I should ask her to marry me (again)!* he thought. Some song came on and Esme pointed upwards at it (as though he was supposed to know), to the rising air – swinging him around, singing *The less we say about it the better* (out of tune), and he remembered her face so close, smiling so ridiculously, the day of champagne and gin and pints and champagne soaked into their skin, her veil disentangling, the zoetrope of half-cut faces bordering them, laughing to each other *This is awkward, isn't it?* Now, their shadows spinning over the floor, the walls, the cupboards. Mara had squidged her playdough Mummy and playdough Daddy and playdough Louis and playdough sheep into a motley ball that she was throwing on to the floor, over and over, laughing. Louis was dazedly, contentedly, staring at them: at Esme and Michael holding each other, laughing and smiling, with all of the distance that love brings, the house huddling over them against the world, when into the kitchen window slapped a sparrow.

Or at least he thought it was a sparrow. Who can identify many birds for certain nowadays? Especially from just the mark they leave on a window . . . The named world is shrinking back into mystery.

It had greased an epithet of itself on the pane: wings spanned, legs split.

*

The clout on the window had made them conscious of the house being around them, with the other houses, as though the bird had been flying from centuries back and unexpectedly found itself out of time. But the song carried on regardless, and Louis began laughing hysterically. Because Louis was laughing, Mara laughed; and Esme, who seemed to be laughing at her own callousness.

It was laid out on the grass, one wing forlorn over its face, humiliated by the suddenness of things. Maybe it was a swift. Regardless, everyone was laughing, except Michael.

He decided to give it a few minutes to cool before he fetched the dustpan and a carrier bag.

13

The tunnel's simplicity broke into sunlight and the complexity of buildings and people and Michael's thoughts were with the pint glasses he'd left on the bar, drained, sea foam. Taking advantage of his parents looking after the kids, he was supposed to meet Esme after his training session in the city, but she'd messaged to say she was catching up with old friends who she hadn't seen forever; he wound up regretting drinking with colleagues instead. He'd drunk off a little of the glumness of his lunchtime expedition to various jewellers to replace the engagement ring he'd imagined out of existence when he first got home (most likely, anyway . . . she might have misplaced it, but he didn't want to raise the subject). None of the shops had anything resembling it, and he began to worry he'd vanished anything of the kind (there'd be some awkward conversations over dinner tables this evening . . .). Those colleagues who hadn't already trailed off laden into the blue evening like bees had headed for karaoke – so Michael escaped to the train home with Julian, who held on to his arm the whole way as though Michael was the only thing stopping him hitting the deck. They crumpled through cans of gin and tonic, burped cheese and pickle sandwiches they'd bought at the station, joked about John retreating early into the evening with his daughter's backpack.

I thought it sounded quite fetching, you know? said Julian.

Michael released a short bolt of a laugh.

Although they were first brought home to the same road in the same year, their names in the same register through school, they'd always been on each other's periphery, Michael and Julian. Never one of the lobbers himself, Julian was mates with the kids who threw things – small stones, empty-ish cans, a dead mouse – at Michael and Luc who, fair enough, wore their haircuts like targets. (It was mostly aimed at Luc on account of almost everything about him, not least the fact that he lived on a farm – at any moment, had he thought of it, Michael could have simply stepped aside and survived unpelted.) Michael and Julian were born six months apart and mostly stayed that way, until those six months Michael fought a losing battle trying to win back his student loan betting on horse-racing – six months that Julian spent going from desert village to desert village with an automatic rifle on a hiding to nothing. Six months that put half the world between them.

Except, here on the train, tipsy and loose-tongued, it was as though they'd been best mates all along, nudging each other with the train's lurch, talking crap about school and football and the office – when Michael, giddy (what was he thinking?), blurted out:

If you could imagine anything out of existence, what would it be?

He must have looked suddenly serious; Julian cleared his throat, stared into his can.

There would be something terrible, thought Michael. Something real. (The footage had smoked through their social networks: the roadside and the dirt, the medic, the helicopter emerging through black air, Julian's voice saying something about a girl. Nobody knew whether to be thankful or suspicious that Julian came out of it all completely unscathed.) Even if the war never seemed real to Michael – seeing the pictures on his phone while he vaped, waiting for the kids to finish their swimming lessons; or leaving the TV to tell the empty room about it while he sliced vegetables in the kitchen – he reckoned you could probably still stick your index finger in the bullet holes on the houses.

Julian was giving it some consideration.

Shit, thought Michael – it was a stupid joke (*you have to be fucking stupid to think you're being clever*); should never have fucking asked, watching this man he sort of knew from school stare into the black hole of a fucking can with fuck-knows-what inside it. Ineffable things. He'd seen dead things, probably made dead things – what if he recognised something in Michael? Something deadening? Terrified, a part of him hoped that he would.

With a kind of silence, Julian looked up into Michael's eyes, and

Mayonnaise, he said. Mayonnaise.

Mayonnaise?

Mayonnaise. What's it move like that for? All like, clumpy. It's disgusting.

Mayonnaise.

⋆

Michael glanced out of the window at the tower-block tors, solid outcrops of sky in their sullen colours, the rain-clouds' hills rolling down on to the houses. Street lamps were waking early, sinking ponds of light into the road. *First they came for the fucking mayonnaise*, he thought . . . with Luc's voice wry in his head, the way he'd brush himself down after the other kids had been throwing things, saying something cutting and pointless, like *So begins the dismantling of Late Capitalism*, ignoring the yoghurt on his trousers.

You?

I dunno. I don't mind mayonnaise. Cats maybe.

I've got a cat.

He couldn't tell if he was joking. He still had that blank, military provision about his apprehension, as though he'd worked out well in advance how to neutralise everything.

Good job I can't imagine things out of existence then, isn't it?

Julian stared at him. Then laughed, once. Hefted himself up, mumbling something about *going for a slash*, passing himself from seat to seat down the aisle.

War. He'd honestly expected him to say *war*. Even after all of the times he'd overheard him laughing in the staff kitchen about getting stopped at airport security for the imaginary shrapnel in his thigh or checking the high street for roadside bombs (disingenuously though, right?). Not that he'd even know where to begin imagining it out of existence.

He wasn't, on second thoughts, even completely sure what guns looked like nowadays, and that was basic war. Helicopters? Frigates? Drones? Fuck knows. He used to be so oblivious to everything – the light would enter the black of his eye, and what did it matter if it was a wave or a particle or both? – he used to be able to sit beside himself on the train window and not think too much about stuff: there was a stone, there was a tree, there were the sodden and fenced-in nameless fields, the caravans on breeze blocks, 4G pitches, a kid's pink tractor sinking into the bank, the car bumper on the mossy lock-up roof, a wind turbine with only two blades and a rusted nose, concrete tubes stacked in mud like hair curlers, all straggled as though the flood of civilisation had receded; now he'd started having those thoughts. The night ones. The overwhelming ones, when there is only the dark and the quiet, animal life of your sleeping wife beside you. Where at least there was her warmth, he thought to himself, her smell. Being by himself was exhausting: trying not to vanish integral things from fear, or boredom. Trying not to, say, look at the track ballast and think how long it will take for the weeds and trees to untangle all this once we're gone, how it will take no time at all. (He'd only gone for a couple of pints, and now this.) Thinking that we don't bring order to the world, that the last thing we do is keep things regulated, stable – we're accelerants, lighter fuel, every little cell of us burning, disturbing things. And all he'd tried to do was narrow the flame, to give some shape to their lives, but. But, what? He didn't know.

Julian was taking his time in the toilet. Michael shuffled in the hard chair; looked out over the backs of the passing houses. He was still chewing his lip when his colleague landed beside him.

I've changed my mind: wasps, he said. Mate, I got stung in the throat once, you know? – almost killed me, he did. They're little arseholes.

Where've you been? asked his mum.

He'd come to pick his kids up but felt as though he was late home from school, the late-evening sun lengthening his hangdog shadow along the path.

She'd answered the door with a glass of wine, squeezing his arm (she was always squeezing him now, like she did to keep him awake at church when he was little in case Grandma noticed). Mara – an Aztec lifeguard – ran to him shouting *Daddy!* and hugged his leg. He tried to ask her about her day, but she was scurrying along the floor after a *Shark! Shark!*

We've been all over the world with our little ladybird here, haven't we, sweetheart? said his mum. She doesn't need us, does she? Sits there gabbing away to herself. What's your friend called? Woolly-bully-something?

Mara didn't answer, too absorbed in whatever was emerging from the carpet. Michael lifted his eyebrows, glanced around.

Where's Louis?

In the garden, his dad shuffled into the conversation. He wouldn't talk to us.

Michael looked through the house to the garden – saw the flower of his son's head dawdling around.

As soon as he was seated, the interrogation began: How did he get here? Was he OK? Could he sleep? How was his appetite? How's Louis' maths? Mara's reading? Did Esme get that text about the article in the Sunday supplement? Was Lucas still seeing that woman from the bank? Why doesn't he think so? Did he see they'd closed the branch on the high street? What other sort of bank is there? Was she one of those? Did he watch the detective programme last night? He didn't? Did he see how much the house went for down the street? Wasn't it a disgrace? They'd be giving them away, next, wouldn't they? Did he want any biscuits? A sandwich? Did Louis' teacher sort it – you know? Was he going to take the kids away somewhere sunny? Couldn't he do with a holiday? Wasn't it driving him mad, being cooped up in there all the time? Well, he didn't think she meant it like that, did he?

The phone burst in and dragged his mum away into a conversation about knitting for the fracking protest. She'd left him to stew in the insufferable, dusky quiet of his dad doing the crossword. He could feel the dust smothering him into the carpet.

Since his dad had given up smoking his voice was clearer, but he still lifted his hand when he spoke as if it was carrying a cigarette, so there was a part of him crumbling towards his lap from a trembling ash-tip. Mum had put a photo from before he was born on the coffee table: Dad with an arm around her, grinning completely by the front door of this home, pregnant with potential. It was like staring into his abyss.

'Almost moony black,' his dad said to himself, ruefully.

Uh?

You seen the hole? his dad asked without looking up.

Yeah – are they finally doing the internet?

His dad shrugged.

Digging my grave, I think.

The newspaper crumpled under his dad's pen. His mum's voice from the kitchen, arguing that they'd knitted too many people chains. Michael remembered how desperate he'd been as a kid, hanging about the house like a saline drip. If he could have visited himself, an apparition in his bedroom, the ghost of Tuesday Future, shown him the house he'd live in around the corner, the conventional family, the job in the offices they were building then just off the bypass, he'd have run out into the street in his Star Wars pyjamas, pleading – *I can change! I can change!*

I'm—

Michael stood, pointed, left the room.

They'd decorated the bathroom again (he'd have to take a tour of it later, pretending he hadn't already been up to pee). Every time he came home they were eager to show him another bit of the house he'd been refurbished from. There wasn't much of his childhood left here, beyond the shadows cast by banisters from the light falling through the open door where Uncle Mike lived for a while (reasons unknown), shifting his things around in a suitcase until he left the country. It was up there that Michael learned a few guitar chords. And how much easier it was to bash the strings while his uncle did all the complicated bits, telling him about dead musicians and black and white films and all the people he was going to get revenge on.

His mum's voice through the floorboards, talking to Rosie or Patricia or Marguerite about *my Michael, who's already flourishing back at work*, made him feel sublimated into some lugubrious figure, creaking in the ceiling. His bedroom was too small and nulled to cramp his eighteen years in it.

A tub of root poison waiting beside him, next door Ron was still hacking away at the tree (*Bless him*, his mum said, *he's been at that since Linda*) that used to block the light when he was little, the roots so thick and entangled that even if he gets it out it'll still continue to grow in their heads. He stopped hacking for a second to watch the train pass. Unexpected, as usual. On their side of the fence, Louis, too, stood up for a moment. He'd turned his dad's old bike upside down by the tiny pond, cranking the back wheel around. It was as though Michael was spying on his childhood self. He could never really remember how he behaved, not properly; there are always stray bits of yourself that dissipate into other things, other people. Watching the boy, Michael wondered of that separate little self – the boy of him that seemed so distant, so cut off by the coma that he could easily refer to him in the third person – what he would get up to; how the both of them (that him, his son) could embody that pronoun almost separately. But

Fucking hell

he was certain he'd never do what he was doing.

★

What's the matter?

Michael didn't stop to answer his mum, running through the kitchen and out into the garden.

Louis!

His son didn't have time to turn around before he'd grabbed his arm.

Louis! Louis! What the hell do you think you're doing?

Michael could hear his father's voice, clattering its cadences back at him off the house. Louis didn't have time to lob a word before the shock throttled him. A small frog still pinched between his finger and thumb.

Louis! Why?

He was still squeezing his arm.

I just . . .

The boy's words came out smeared, teary.

. . . just wanted to see what would happen.

He fell from his dad's grip and ran back into the house, squirming past Grandma at the backdoor, there to see what all this fuss was about.

Tiny frogs were breast-stroking around the pond where his dad used to stunt carp, a few lounging around the mossy stone wall at its edge. The bike wheel's scythe began to slow; through the grey whir, in the grass, you could see frog legs, frog torsos.

What's all this crying about?

Michael imagined his son growing up to be one of those psychopaths that doesn't so much blame his parents in the courtroom, but lets the story of his childhood speak for itself. Whenever he imagined him killing, though, he could only see his boy's face on a strange man's body, terrified at what it was doing.

Holding Louis felt like he was holding something trapped. (The jibbing calf Lucas's dad shouted at them for not pinning down properly, trapped into being. He had a weathered stump of a voice, Lucas's dad: *Fuck's sake, grab it, the pair of you! Three fucking useless boys.* (It was only when he got home that Michael realised who the third 'boy' was, and what was going to happen to him.) Was it the only time he went round? He remembered Jack and Whatshisface shouting *Barnhead* at Luc, throwing muck at him. Michael worried they'd somehow seen him pin down the calf, too. He never said a word.)

Well, what's the matter?

The calf's pond-black eye, nearly the size of its head.

He turned the bike the right way up, wheeled it towards the shed.

Nothing, Mum.

12

The other day at Mum's, Louis was—

Michael didn't know how to phrase it. He'd left it roiling in his mind for a few days. Esme, late home from work again, was scrolling through her phone as she lifted a forkful of risotto spilling to her mouth.

Being a bit weird.

How d'you mean? she said, without looking up.

I dunno.

(On his lunch, or an extended version of it, taking liberties with his post-coma recuperation, Michael had walked as usual to the scrutty wood by the motorway. Between sad bites of his salad and useless scrolls in search of an engagement ring, he held back the flood that would engulf their house; imagined the river's murky afterwater loitering in their living room; the scumline of its surge at Mara's height, the height she was when the river carried her away, how he lifts her drowsy body upstairs to sleep.

For a while he sat there, staring at the puddle in the tyre scut where someone had driven through the track, the dinge of it. Beneath the lower growth, by the lungwort and wood spurge, by the crisp packets and the condom, lay a bird. Michael looked up to the trees, as though there might be some solid explanation for it falling out of the sky. The waft of the canopy felt dismissive. The bird was expressionless, or beyond expression. It had all the certainty of the past tense: the simple fact of a bird, stripped of being's complications and fluidities – that constant twitchiness of becoming bird, of the heartbeat's insistence on proving itself. He wondered if he could bring it back to life and laughed.

Then thought about it seriously.

He wasn't entirely sure where to begin – imagined it being eaten back into the forest floor, the coral scorch of its plump chest fading into the muddier brown of the leaf-fall, those coal-glossed wings breaking apart into flies, maggots prising from its bullet-tip beak . . . But decomposition isn't the opposite of life; it's the churn of it. No matter how hard he concentrated, he couldn't bring the life back to that dead bird. He could sense its nothingness. The way sometimes you can sense someone staring at you on the train or in the checkout queue.

Michael poked the bird with a stick, as though he might nudge it alive. And how the dead speak in the voices of the living, that black eye stared back him: *You dick.*)

So here he was at the dinner table, raising the subject of his son, a dead bird on his mind. The clash of his post-coma homecoming had taken a few weeks to settle into the lovely, messy noise of a family. Now he worried Esme was slackening from them. Half-interested, not recognising the inflection in her husband's voice, that there was something he wanted her to pick up on, she asked him *How d'you mean?* Michael didn't want to feel like he was grassing on his own son – only partly because he felt complicit. Only partly because he'd walked back to his desk that afternoon to answer phone calls from solicitors representing people with hand-arm vibration as though he hadn't spent a long lunch trying to imagine a bird back to life.

He's fine – he was just in a bit of a strange mood, that's all.

Esme shrugged, typing a message with her forkless hand.

What are you so busy with, anyway?

I'm just messaging Luc. I'm gonna write a book, she smiled.

Oh yeah, he said. What about?

The end of the world.

Great, when is it?

She gave his joke a withering look, like she couldn't remember exactly how she'd ended up with this imbecile.

About prophecies and oracles and collapses and now, she said. How everything's screwed. You are taking them to gymnastics tomorrow night, aren't you?

(He'd imagined the kids snapping their thin arms, their thin legs, their too, too thin necks.)

We're going to a lecture on Corippus at the Institute, so I won't get back till late.

Yeah, he mumbled, yeah.

Thinking to himself *The end of the fucking world.* So blithe, as though her only responsibility was the quality of soil she left behind. She wasn't being herself; he knew that attachment – the way the kids rooted them into the future. (He didn't know where to begin.) But then he couldn't tell where his amnesia ended and Esme's confidentiality began. When he tried to think of anyone in her family other than Alex, they were disassembled faces – the ghosts of accents that Esme and her sister had, by the sounds of things, buried far down. Was that what she was doing here, with him – hiding? It was as though she had this other, frail life, an ineffable life, too precarious to be touched into daylight. An image bruised in his mind – somewhere deep that cared about his place in everything: Esme, holding hands on the beach, the sun setting beneath a wall of ocean. But not with him.

11

It doesn't take much. Sometimes you can just be sulking by the driving range after you've had an argument with your wife about whether you should imagine her dying of cancer again, because *What if you didn't get it right?* (there are only so many times you can curl into the camping chair in the shed, crying, because it feels like she's actually dead, like your son's actually dead, your daughter), which was really a manufactured argument about something else entirely, something that couldn't (or daren't) be brought into words – so you are just sulking by the driving range, watching the meteor shower of passable shots.

For a man who could imagine things out of existence, he felt uniquely powerless. He'd been worrying about Esme. It worried him that he could worry. It's not like she would die or anything – not soon, anyway. But he'd try to catch her somewhere, after the kids were in bed, say, at the fridge filling her glass – he'd touch her hips; she'd flinch. She always flinched now – as though her body, preconsciously, had felt something struggling into thoughts. *It's someone walking over your grave, that is.* The future's past tense. When they managed to have sex, he wasn't altogether there – too heightened, too anticipatory. He was remembering her, the windfall of hair on her collarbone as she undressed, the red flush on her chest that first time (*I've forgotten half my life*, he thought, *but I haven't forgotten that*). And other women, with less subtlety, too, if he was honest. But it never felt quite right; felt like a deprivation. When they'd finished, she always rolled straight over to her phone and left him lying there in the past, damply.

A cyclist sank by the road along the driving range (the clicking freewheel reminded him of his granddad, trapping moths in matchboxes because he liked the sound of them battering the cardboard). Too late to catch sight, Michael wondered if it could have been Luc. Apparently he'd been riding out this way more recently, skirting across the surface of their childhood. He chuckled, noticing himself thinking, *I wouldn't, bit dangerous these roads.* Luc would thunder downhill here, crouched over the top tube, blithe to anyone pulling out on to the road. He'd always been so confident about everything. *I wonder if he ever has a boring day?* Esme said. The glee on her face; he remembered the sight of them emerging from the festival crowd (he'd lost her somewhere, no phone signal, chewing his knuckles for hours), Esme piggybacking on Luc, her bare feet frogged out, laughing as his wellies chomped through the thick gouts of mud, rescued, a happiness spilling from her that seemed so much greater than the well he'd found.

He sighed, fearing what else his amnesia had in store for him. Golf balls shot off as though an ambitious popcorn enterprise had gone awry. His whole life felt ludicrous as he tried not to think about Esme. He tried not to think about anything, watching a magpie stab its head into a yoghurt pot, liberated from the overflowing bin. It scuffed along, flicking raindrops. Eventually managed to scoop the pot on to its side – but, before it knew what had happened, it jabbed clean through, wedged its beak into it; this white, fragrant world pulled suddenly down over its eyes.

Idiot, said Michael, feeling a little better about himself.

A sullen, slow walk home, back through the holloway. He thought about asking Esme if he could stop imagining things. It was enough; they were safe. (When he was little, Uncle Mike gripped on to him so he could lean over a cliff – once he realised he wouldn't fall, the sea-thrill of all that gravity and rock receded to a nauseous anxiety – *What if he got tired, or distracted, or bored, and dropped me?*) He wanted to keep things as they were. Or ideally, as they were a few weeks ago, when he and Esme would curl up into each other on the sofa, the kids asleep upstairs, and everything felt suspended. So he'd retreat to the shed and try to keep things as they are by changing the future, by feeling his wife's death, his kids' deaths. And, stepping out from the shed, it was as though he could sense the nothing around and between them, between his atoms, the mostly empty space of solid things. As though they were gauze people, his family – unreal, in a gauze garden, with gauze birds. And the countless tiny particles of actual existence tickling through the mesh of them. A net, trawled through the world, lifting what little life they could.

And now it was getting dark on his walk and he worried his family would slip from him through the gaps. Far off he could see the lone headlamp of a long-distance runner, mining distance from the woods. There was nowhere you could be alone any more – not properly, not here. His feet sulked though the mulch, a rumour of drizzle chattering among the leaves. He wondered from what far ocean the clouds had formed, holding his hand out from his pocket to let the rain rest in his palm, and imagined it stopping.

Oh no! said Mara, halfway down the stairs in her pyjamas. The sky fell over on to Daddy!

Bloody hell, Michael – you could've messaged me!

Esme shouted from the dark kitchen. He'd dripped through the door, the whole of him being pulled wetly towards the ground. As he unsocketed his feet from the sodden shoes, Esme shuffled Mara back up to bed, coaxing her imaginary friend Bellywoollen with her.

You're sodden, she said, shaking her head. Why didn't you just imagine yourself without an umbrella?

How many times?! It doesn't work that way, he said, as though he knew exactly how it worked. Don't you think I've imagined myself not driving a Ferrari?

His socks chomped down the corridor to the kitchen; she was in the bronzeglare of her computer, a Gorgonzola sandwich beside her, the pitched roof of a book, and a glass of burgundy.

I thought you were being practical for once, she said. You wouldn't suit a Ferrari anyway. You're a bit too—, she waved her hand vaguely in his direction, for a Ferrari.

What?

You know.

He sensed she was considering a nicer way of putting it.

Blue.

Blue?

The blueness bruising back into the skin beneath his nails, those lunar knuckles, the skin under his eyes.

Yeah – you know what I mean.

He couldn't control it. His hair was shivering greasy splotches on to the table where he leaned beside her, the deep-set cold beginning to sting into the warmth of the house.

Greyish blue, ocean coloured, stolid, like a manatee or a—

Esme, he interrupted. I can't keep imagining you dying of things. I shouldn't have blown my lid earlier, but I can't keep doing it. It feels so real –

Michael –

I can't cope with it. It feels like I've only just found you and now I'm having to—

Michael!

What?

You're dripping water everywhere.

You're dripping water everywhere! she'd said. They were slushdrunk and covered in field muck, trying to undress inside and outside of their tent simultaneously. (It was her idea: camping far north in winter to try and catch the aurora, almost catching pneumonia.) *Es*, he said, holding up, torch-lit, the hoodie she'd been using as a makeshift pillow: saturated, where the inner web of the tent had kissed the outer skin and the whole day of rain came drenching through. *Oh crap*, she laughed – he vaguely remembered she laughed – before crumpling on top of him, giggling in the wet mess of their things.

He smiled – opened himself up for a hug. She touched his chest, tentatively – flinched.

Seriously, you're soaking. Go and get changed.

Sorry.

Undressing along the hallway, up the stairs, he imagined her being hit by a bus, falling into the river, sitting at her bedside while the doctors shook their heads. It didn't make him feel happier, but it felt like an act of love.

10

Instead of picturing the kids falling from skyscrapers, Michael had spent his working day reading about the earthquake in Mexico. All afternoon, the ringing phones sounded like small cries under the rubble of chatter. In the traffic jam on the way home (that he chose not to imagine), he listened to them talking about it on the news, the soft rain making him think of a detuned radio, alone in a half-crumbled room. He wanted to make a hero of himself, imagining little Frida Sofía and her schoolmates covered in dust. But Esme, towel wrapped around her head and applying mascara, had already made her point clear enough when the typhoon struck: *You'd only fuck it up.* How do you know the tigers aren't just hiding in your imaginary jungle? What does methane even look like? His imaginative skills were the equivalent of turning up to a war zone with a dustpan and brush. And it wasn't that she lacked empathy, but she'd watched a documentary about rising populations and found it hard to worry about statistical deaths. She kept on about the Plague of Athens – at bedtime, at dinnertime, on the school run – as though it was a Mediterranean cruise. *A Dorian war will come*, she announced at the school gates in stentorian voice when Mrs Shuttle had mentioned that bother over the drone strikes, *and with it, a plague.* So really it was no surprise, the look she gave his plea to help the stricken children: that wry eyebrow seeming to say, *Imagine some of us out of existence* – as though he was blessed with a distinct lack of imagination. She didn't even know about the speed camera on his way to work, or the branch that squirrel was sitting on.

But, half-watching the clear-up on the evening news while checking her phone, her feet resting on Michael's thighs, Esme wondered,

Did you actually imagine me with lung cancer?

Yeah.

She took a deep breath, exhaled.

I don't feel any less cancerous.

Well you wouldn't, would you?

She gave him a sour look.

Shouldn't you be able to feel it, though – don't you think?

I can. It's shit.

Shit? *Shit* how?

Shit like— I dunno.

A loss, he wanted to say. A grief compacted: the way you lose a whole childhood when a goldfish dies. But it was ridiculous, when (physically, at least) he felt almost nothing – a slight faintness, a slight headache.

Why d'you think I'm in a sulk every time I do it?

Well, you're just a bit moody, aren't you?

There was always this undertone, whenever she asked if he'd imagined things: it was never enough. She could go further, had gone further. He could imagine terrible things, she could imagine the absolute worst. The unspeakable. He'd just been born again to a wife he loved, children he loved, and he'd barely had to suffer for them. Could barely remember the accumulation of worries and mistakes, the arguments, the reconciliations that go into domesticating. That they'd pushed parts of her aside – kidneys, bladder, lungs – to come into this world, and now she could feel, inside her, the visceral terror of the space they'd leave behind.

I don't believe you, she said.

Uh? But, the brick, and—

No, it's not that I don't believe you. I want to feel it.

Feel it?

She stared at him, inscrutably. Then she put her wine glass down and hurried off to the kitchen.

Esme?

When she returned, there was a knife in her hand and a serious look on her face.

Imagine me with a cut on my hand.

What the— Esme?

Right here. Across my palm.

Don't be ridiculous.

It won't be a massive one. Just imagine me cutting myself.

I'm not going to imagine that.

Why not?

A chuckle coughed out of him, as though he could joke the whole thing away. But she was clenched still, her whole body transformed into the thought of running the knife across her palm.

Are you serious? This is insane, Esme.

Fuck off. Don't give me that bullshit. I want to feel it.

What d'you mean? You probably won't feel anything. I—

I want to know it. It's not enough to fucking sit here and hypothesise that you can erase things with your mind. I need to feel it, Michael. To feel it's true.

Uh?

This wasn't the Esme he had expected this evening. This was – he didn't know what it was.

But what about the brick? Max?!

Bricks! This is our kids. This is them not falling, or getting ill, or being hit or kidnapped or— Do it. Come on.

But – just put the knife down, Es – you've seen it.

He was waiting for her to crack into a laugh; she didn't. She stared at him, testing, unfamiliar.

Are you scared you can't do it? Is that it?

No. I don't know. I don't see why this is a good idea.

Don't you want to know? Don't you want to see you can do it?

I have!

What about here instead then?

She lined the knife along a vein in her forearm.

Oh, come on Esme.

What? Nothing will happen, will it? It's not as though I'd bleed to death.

Don't.

Why not?

Don't.

Imagine me cutting myself open.
Seriously Esme, don't mess about.
Do it.
Come on, Es.
Do it.
Esme—

A slice, upwards – she bent over herself with a gasp.

Esme!

Then a little yelp. She was gripping her arm; the knife dropped on to the floor. He rushed over to her. He couldn't see anything, crouched like that, her hair fallen like that.

When she stood up her face was scrunched. There wasn't a mark on her. She crumpled again, into laughter.

You should've seen your face!

It's not funny.

What, did you really think I was going to cut myself?

It's not funny.

He picked the knife up; there wasn't a hint of blood on it.

Shitting hell, Esme.

Louis was pyjama-quiet in the doorway, peeping: Mummy crouched against the wall, shuddering, tears in her eyes, laughter; Daddy standing over her, holding a knife.

Oh, hello mate, did you wake up?

The boy stared. Esme lifted her hair from her face, stifled her sputters for a moment.

Are you OK lovely? Did Mummy and Daddy wake you up playing games?

She crawled over to him with the last of her giggles, lifted him up – a grunty sigh sounding her age. Kissed his cheek; carried him at her shoulder.

Do you want a biscuit? Or one of Mummy's special tuck-ins?

He didn't say a thing; stared at Daddy, who was staring at the living-room floor, one hand holding his head, the other holding a knife.

Don't mind Daddy, she said too loudly, he's just an imbecile.

The knife didn't say a word.

9

Saturday morning, and Michael chuntered damply from the shed, lifting his head from the shipwrecks, the localised tsunamis, their bodies afloat, face down, in various swimming pools. Now Mara was too busy for swimming: Bellywoollen had called a *board meeting* and all the important toys and others were in attendance. Including Louis, but he was too busy to notice, malaising aristocratically about the house.

What are you doing stuck in here?

Michael was pointing to the window as if to say *There's a world outside, explore!* In the way his dad had nagged him. Louis lay cat-stretched and yawning on the couch.

I'm in a coma.

Well how come you're talking?

He gave him a joshing shove.

I'm not talking.

Pushed him harder, groaning to the floor.

You're rubbish at this game. Go outside. Play football.

Louis rolled his eyes towards the raindrops exhausting themselves on the window.

I'm bored.

Set fire to something then. Throw stones at pensioners. Lay traps for cats.

Wouldn't I go to prison?

Michael thought back to Louis in his parents' garden, the frogs, telling him off on the way home – *You'll end up in prison, carrying on like that!* It left a thick residue in his throat, an overreaction, a self-consciousness. The way they show up your own behaviour so clearly, so impressionably. The sight of Louis in the rear-view mirror: red grass marks scored into his shins, the red rims of his eyes.

Well we can't afford to feed you both, and Mara eats less.

Louis sighed.

But it'll be even more boringer in prison.

More boring. They'll let you get a tattoo in prison.

I don't want a tattoo.

I thought you wanted a tattoo of your times tables?

No, said Louis disgusted.

Oh, I remember it was the teacher you were going to get – what's her name?

Louis tutted.

Why don't you see if you can climb on to the roof? It'll be good training for when you're in prison.

What's the point? It's not like I'm going to fall off.

He lay there, his head hanging upside down off the sofa, eyes rolled towards the floor. Defeated, his dad nodded.

Except, Michael stood dizzily in the hallway, looking over the list Esme had given him for tomorrow – malaria, male pattern baldness, falling masonry – a mothy sweat encroaching his neck. It wasn't like the boy was going to fall off the roof – he was just going to lie there listless as though there was no point to it, as though it meant nothing to throw the lives of small frogs into a spinning wheel, because what did a frog mean? Or a bird? Or a boy? It wasn't like he was going to fall off at all.

Esme!

Unsure light lifted the hallway almost into brighter air. The blood flushed back; he crumpled the list in his pocket. Trooping upstairs, he shouted

Esme! Esme!

with an unassailable determination that they were going to the beach. (That was sunlight approaching through their bedroom window.) The sea wind – it'd lift them from their stupor, reinvigorate them, restore them to being that family he rediscovered from the blankness of his coma, the one that only a month or so ago (was it that recent?) had set out to the river and the hills as though they'd discovered them. And he wouldn't imagine the car exploding or a tidal wave devouring them or a shark dragging any of them from the ankle-depths into the unreachable dark. They'd be fine! (*They would be fine?*) The sea, he'd learned from the TV rescue programmes, is dangerously unpredictable. Its risk would sharpen them back to each other, make them feel the need of each other. The sea!

Esme had never hidden her hatred of sand: it smothered and weathered, secreted itself perniciously. He hadn't finished talking (*We're festering in here*) by the time she'd conceded, twice, a touch stunned by his new love of seashells, brinestinks and pierwood-damp. She couldn't remember marrying this ecstatically coastal man. (In fact, she confessed later that day that she could barely remember their wedding day at all, blaming the amnesia of nerves and booze. Even though the world kept beguiling him with wedding memories – blossom, swans, cascading bells – and not once did she seem drunk or anxious. He supposed some people hide things better than others.) Louis groaned and asked if he could at least bring his friend Joseph from a few doors down. Mara requested Bellywoollen postpone their board meeting.

While he was buttering bread for a picnic that Esme knew would only find itself in a beachfront bin, she dug a finger into his side.

You have imagined them drowning, haven't you? Being swept out to sea?

He blenched away from her.

I'm going to throw them in the sea and not imagine them drowning.

He smiled, as if he was only joking. She shook her head, agitated.

All the doors were thrown open, the breeze was hurrying everything on as though the beach might disappear.

Don't play with your ball in the road, Louis.

Whatever the boy's answer (something about his friend), Michael was distracted. Standing outside on the path, holding Mara's hand as Esme popped in to fetch the other car seat, a bird smacked the floor beside him; after a cataleptic second, the magpie scrabbled on the path outside their house, trying to lever itself up from the floor with a wing and on to its feet.

What's wrong, Daddy?

I think it's hurt.

Birds' shadows faltered across the pavement, across the parked cars where Louis had gone to call for Joe, but when he looked up to the sky – packed grey ceiling insulation – there was no sign. Sun-blinded, Michael could just about hear some other birds, disquieting. Maybe there'd been a fight, but the look in its eye was as though it had just forgotten how to fly. He crouched to lift its scrawling body when Mara screeched

Joseph!

The car screeched, too.

The ball made four gently diminishing hops towards the other side of the road, where Louis lifted it from the floor.

Esme had tumbled downstairs to find her husband stunned on the pavement, their stunned daughter. Between the tyre marks, with barely a breath, Joseph stood, his arms out in front of him as though he still might catch the ball.

Esme rushed to him.

The driver glared at Michael (gawping there with a dead bird in his hands) with a *he just ran out – there was nowhere to go* look on her face, except where she went hadn't touched the boy. Clutching her blouse at her chest, the look she gave him: as if they were in on it together.

By now Joseph's dad had come tumbling out. Michael threw the bird over the fence and shuffled to them. The boy was perfectly intact, but his face suggested he didn't know what hadn't hit him.

Are you OK, Joe?

What happened?

He wheezed a few little screeches. Blinked back to himself. Louis dawdled over to him and handed him the ball.

Are you all right, Joe?

The houses all looked at each other for answers. Eventually, the driver managed to move again – came to make emergency small talk. Everyone was OK. Everything was fine. Mara held a private chat with Bellywoollen by the kerb amid the corroborative chuntering. Michael wiped the bird grease on his jeans. The car sat with its engine turning over, panting; a wag of exhaust fumes hid into the air.

I got run over, said Joseph, when they were almost at the seaside.

He'd dismissed the whole thing with the insouciance of a child. Which is to say that he let it clot somewhere deep and innocuous in his emotional vasculature, ready to bring the whole operation gasping to the floor at some point down the line.

Hhhhmmm, said Michael, I don't think you did Joe. I think it was just a close call.

The seaside wasn't as he'd remembered. But the seaside only exists as a static thing in the memory; its buildings fade, the land and sea arguing over the same bit of neither. Gusts huffed every now and then, pulling the ropes on the upturned boats, belching up sand. Meanwhile, pensioned seagulls paraded up and down the shore.

It wasn't one of those days where you could lounge on the beach; they all had to keep moving. At the pier's end, the sea frustrated between the slats, Louis tapped his dad's leg and asked *Will you throw me off?* and then sulked because

Daddy used to be fun. The kids had fallen out over whose idea it was to dig a hole. When they stopped to eat on a bench with the wind in their faces, Mara cried because there was sand in her peanut-butter sandwich and she had to be bargained down from an ice cream each for her and Bellywoollen to one they could share. Then she cried because their mouths were too cold. The boys had given up eating and were passing the ball to each other as though each was elsewhere, and for what felt like five minutes Mara was satisfied with her mound of sand. She came blubbering across the few feet of freedom they'd given her – trying to explain something about falling out – having to stop, whining, stuttering her breath – falling out with Bellywoollen over a crab, when Esme blurted out

Bellywoollen's not real!

She looked exasperated, as though all this had been forced on her, this child, this husband – they were all idiots. Couldn't they keep their stupidities private?

Michael lifted his crying daughter and carried her over to the rock pools.

Shall we hunt some crabs, then fish and chips after – yeah?

Joe was kicking the ball at a static Louis, running after it himself. Esme was glowering at the sea, its accountability. Holding Mara over the sand, her head buried into his shoulder, Michael imagined them all screaming at each other. Imagined the family breaking into acrimony and lawyers as he walked towards the rock pools by the mottled, kelp-draggled underbelly of the pier.

Look at this one! he said, pointing to the sand-sludged thing, grappling into the pool the way he thought fatherhood moves you: submerged and sideways into the same place. Its slow tide of delusion that leaves you comparing yourself to a crab.

Wow!

The pier laughed its damp wooden laugh, off the end into the sea.

With Mara settled, Michael sat beside his wife. He'd considered trying to win a tacky engagement ring at the arcades, only partly as a joke, but thought better of it. (The imagined scene, where he was on one knee, struggling to open the plastic packet the pinky-blue ring came in, at least prevented Esme from actually kicking him in the face.) Anyway, her half-smile said all that either of them needed: a slight apology, but more an acknowledgement that the sea hadn't brought them the perfect day they'd envisaged. It was the ghostly rotations of wind turbines. Gulls trying to leverage themselves against the gusts. Drizzle blown over the tops of their heads.

He remembered how different it seemed as a kid, the sea: unthinkably big and monstrously stupid. That grey day, the rain spattering the car window, when Mum and Dad locked him in there with the radio on for what felt like ages (he turned it off, listened to the sea's sound, dull as traffic) then came back with Uncle Mike, wheezing in a blanket, completely soaked. What had he gone swimming in his normal clothes for? They gave him a flask of tea and he smiled at his nephew, an unexpected presence. Little Michael sulked all the way home because they didn't even get fish and chips or anything.

⋆

Michael, she said, mithered at him taking another photo of the kids playing. It's unhealthy, she added.

She was always photographing them! Or used to, anyway. But he didn't want to start another argument. Fine, they needed to forget themselves to grow up. And he understood why she'd deleted everything off his phone – or he said he did – but now he wanted to keep as much of the kids as he could. He wasn't entirely sure that she didn't see him sinking in a hospital bed and want a blank slate.

He pulled himself deeper into his coat.

Bucolic, isn't it?

Esme raised her eyebrow at his earnestness, pointing to the queue of oil tankers waiting on the horizon for a good price. They'd given up trying to get decent internet signal and were looking out to the sea instead. It was still flattish and pretending to join the sky.

Joe seems to have recovered, said Michael. Looked like he'd completely forgotten how to breathe.

Nature is clamouring for two things only, said Esme in a low voice: a body free from pain and a mind released from worry and fear.

I worried he'd shat himself.

Lucretius.

No, Joe.

The stubborn front she'd held against him broke a little, as though she'd remembered the man she loved. She held his arm, nuzzled, squinting against the sandy light, the sea's glare. Like this, they were cooling on a sunlit balcony somewhere, once, after a blazing row. He couldn't remember exactly what it was about (oversleeping, or lunch, something like that), because it wasn't about that at all.

It was their argument: that argument, so unnameable, that its only inflections are spats over dirty cups, bad directions, misspent afternoons. Where she could feel needed and appreciated, where he could feel needed and validated. The pair of them, sitting there, sharing a doughnut, in the silence that binds the notes.

She pulled away from him.

You shouldn't have done it, she said.

What?

Joe.

What?

It was too risky.

Are you serious?

. . .

What? I should've just let him get run over?

If somebody finds out, we're finished – you do know that?

Come on . . . We'd be better off if Joe got hit by that car?

She shrugged, indifferent.

Bloody hell, Esme.

We're not sharks.

You might be, the look he gave her said.

We need our anxieties.

Except when it comes to your kids.

Except when it comes to mine. Anyway . . . she said, brushing her hand through his hair, conciliatory, but also as though she was peeling back the layers. We have our anxiety right here.

He raised an eyebrow. Leaned her head on his shoulder, looking out to sea; the unquiet arcades behind them, seagulls lobbing their ropey voices into the offing.

But you still get to be a hero, though. My little Herakles, she said, rubbing his meagre bicep only slightly mockingly.

I love you, he said, putting his arm around her.

She yawned, saying I love you, too.

She laughed at herself. Sea air, she said.

He thought again about the arcade engagement ring, accosting her on the pier – she might have loved it, the spontaneity, the kitsch of it – silly, and lovely, and. And it could never happen, now.

Let's go home, he said assertively.

Neither of them moved.

8

Call it a coincidence, but after a drool of an emergency day off (on the sofa, mostly) because Louis was *too poorly* to go to school (there was nothing wrong with him, but Michael remembered the occasional day when he pretended to be sick as a kid and thought it might do Louis some good), a day that he spent doing a jigsaw of Vermeer's *Gentleman washing his hands in a see-through room* (he found piecing the blank space with its absolute rules comforting, even if Luc had declared his love for jigsaws *a fascist pastime*, or, more accurately, *a fucking fascist pastime*), and after a tuna-salad lunch with the boy (who was supine, now, on the carpet, watching YouTube select videos of other kids opening things) and an afternoon where he lay on the sofa to watch the cycling or, more accurately, let the cycling happen while he stared at the mountains and lakes, there was an untimely knock at the door.

What happened to your eye?

Luc had a plaster over his temple and the stain of a black eye.

The road rash on my arse is worse. Fell off my bike the other week.

Shit, said Michael. How did that happen?

Didn't Esme tell you? No fucking idea, Luc shrugged. One second you're upright, the next you're sliding along the floor.

He had a vision of Esme tending to him, daubing his skin, sopping cotton wool in a little bowl of antiseptic so gently you'd think it had feelings.

D'you want a drink then?

Michael had barely heard from Luc since they went for dinner – what, five? six? weeks ago. His friend's coat dripped from the banister as he raced Louis on a video game. If it wasn't for the way he didn't quite seem to know why he'd come round, or the way Louis cared less about racing than crashing his car as catastrophically as possible (repeatedly), you'd say it was a wholesome scene. They never called him Uncle Luc because Esme was pernickety about definitions, but Michael felt as though it might have, in some way, made things better, or easier, if they had.

Where's Es?

He'd already asked once.

Working late.

Luc kept giving him heavy looks, as if he was trying to elicit information. There was a sickly panic that Esme had told him everything, or that he'd worked it (mostly) out – the way he managed to work out that Michael had *borrowed* the BB gun from Luc's loft (there were pockmarks on the tree over the back of Michael's fence aligning exactly with the firing angle from his bedroom window, and the gun was there on his bed when Luc came round). But he couldn't have known about the stapler he'd vanished at work to wind up John, or felt all crisp packets and bottles and other detritus disappearing from the woods, or that Esme and the kids were completely untouchable or that he'd imagined him riding his bike perfectly well. Or that right now, guiltily, Michael was picturing him sleeping badly; his wounds healing slowly; his insurance not paying out; Esme, bedside in the hospital, crying. How strangely we exist in the heads of others. Whatever *Michael* moved through that mind of Luc's, doing indecipherable things, moved in a vocabulary outside his own.

Mara came demanding a bedtime story from Luc: Belly-woollen chose a tale about a missing bear and non-uncle Luc did all the voices. Michael was clearing the kitchen, listening to the story sink through the ceiling, in the galley of his own life, wondering if that sound upstairs would have moved in permanently if the golf ball had hit him a little harder?

And as he was tidying things away – the kids having torn through the place with the indiscretion of secret police – the crayons, toy dinosaurs, the motley ball of playdough as dense as a planet, he heard Mara's voice shout:

Daddy can disappear things!

The floorboards creaked. That faint yellow stain on the ceiling had spread.

Daddy can disappear things, can he? said Luc's muffled voice. I can disappear things, too. Watch.

Michael stared at the ceiling.

A few seconds later, Mara's laughter came flooding through the floor. Luc began reading the story again.

Michael must have inadvertently imagined the playdough from his hand, his palm squeezing empty air.

It was dark at the door, the porch light sparking a brief moment in the drizzle's fall. Luc had lasted one-third of a bottle of beer in relative silence before he declared it was time to go.

I feel like we don't see each other any more, he said in the doorway, as though he'd waited for exactly the wrong moment.

Busy lives, mate.

Yeah, but . . .

Luc brushed back his dampening hair.

It's ridiculous – I knew more about what was going on with you when you were laid out in hospital like a fucking Sunday roast.

To be fair, I didn't have much going on.

I think I preferred you comatose.

Yeah, me too. Simpler times.

Seriously though, what's going on with you?

Michael looked at the evening incredulously.

I'm watching you getting wet.

Luc gave a wry smile, nodded, conceding.

Are you sure you don't want to stay for dinner, or at least until Esme gets back?

No, I should probably head off.

Speak of the devil, said Michael.

Esme approached, her pale face luminous between the dark coat and the umbrella, ending a phone call with her sister.

What are you doing here?! she smiled.

Just leaving.

You're not even staying for dinner?

No, I—

Luc pointed vaguely in the direction of the train station, looking at her as though he wanted to say something else and couldn't. Or didn't have the words. A hug and a kiss from Esme came with her holding the umbrella awkwardly over their heads, the porch light momentarily pulling a white veil of drizzle around them. A nod, a wave, and Luc hunched his shoulders into the dark.

How come he was here?

Esme was shaking the raindrops from her umbrella outside, one step into the house. She seemed anxious about Luc having been.

Dunno, said Michael. He just came around. D'you fancy quiche for dinner?

She nodded indifferently – mentioned something about having work to do, was typing a message on her phone.

Louis is fine by the way, he said, trying to snag her attention on the way up the stairs.

She stopped mid-step, looked over her shoulder at him: a look that made Michael so apparent to himself, since it was perfectly obvious Louis was fine because her husband had obliterated every illness imaginable from his future – her strange, unrecognisable husband, who stood at the bottom of the stairs trying to make her feel bad about missing an hour or two of her children's lives, when she was the one who gave birth to them, who fed them from her own body, a look as though she couldn't remember him being there when it mattered. He went to apologise and already she was up the next step. By the time she reached their bedroom, the rain by the porch had slipped into the dark.

★

Mara was still awake. Conspiring with a torch under her duvet. And when Michael delicately lifted it back, she looked up at him like a crab from under its rock.

The moon's so stupid, she said. Why doesn't it fall down and crush the house?

It doesn't work like that, said Michael, but he struggled to explain exactly why. It was exhausting to think. The image of it falling through the roof crashed on him anyway.

She tucked herself in and refused another story. He wanted to say to her, *Daddy can't make things disappear, you know.* But whatever it was – the lie, the truth – he couldn't bring himself. It didn't sound right in the third person. It didn't sound right in the first. But, in an effort to feel fatherly, he nuzzled a cuddly toy to her cheek. The first that came to hand. It was Louis'. And she'd—

Mara, what did you do to Mr Leonard?

And Fluffles. Squidgy. She'd done it to all of them, hers, her brother's: their seams split, their insides gored out.

Bellywoollen wanted to see what was in there.

Mara, you shouldn't do that. You— he had to think of a moral imperative. You have to look after your toys.

She scowled at him, as though it was none of his business.

Daddy, he hesitated. Daddy can't make things disappear.

She looked, clearly, at the idiot in him.

I can, she said. I made Louis disappear. I'll show you. Not now. I'm going to sleep now.

She pulled the duvet over her head.

OK, Mara.

He tucked her in properly, thinking *Daddy can't. Daddy can't.*

★

And later, when Esme was downstairs watching TV and he was sure Mara was asleep, he crept into her room.

I'm sorry, he whispered. I can really.

The girl's eyelids fluttered, palely; his breath shallow, Michael imagined standing at her hospital bedside, six weeks into a coma, the rain trying to pass through the window. If only he could see what she was dreaming.

7

For too many sensible reasons, imagining the manky tennis ball that the mackintosh woman's terrier had chased into the bushes didn't make him feel any better – not even when the dog re-emerged with that confounded *I-swear-to-God* look on its face. It reminded him of Max. And he felt bad for the woman when she waded in to look with her jacket sleeves pulled over her hands, toeing at the grasses – and found himself pretending to look, too. So the long walk home from work that was supposed to clear his mind didn't. The lanes were sodden. The traffic behind the curtain of trees insistent. His shoes were covered in muck. *Just out for a walk?* she'd asked. He didn't know how to answer.

The world outside was riddled with cancer and car accidents and debt and women whose dogs' tennis balls had gone missing, and he just wanted to be inside with his wife and his children where nothing bad ever happened.

So he did it. (It'd stop things unravelling.) He stood outside his house and imagined Esme and Luc kissing. Her leading him up the stairs. To that bedroom. There. Where, half-undressed, flushed, she would come to the window, with a brief glance across the road, where her husband wouldn't be looking back, and close the curtains.

Stepping through the door, he felt grotty but relieved, somehow, like he'd pulled out some festering toenail. Joseph's mum was here, *just leaving*, eating a biscuit at the kitchen table. He could see Esme was trying to be caring and interested, even with her phone thrumming from emails and messages.

Esme was just telling me about her sister – it's such a shame, isn't it?

Yeah, said Michael, er—

Thinking *You what?* and that it would have felt really nice to curl up on the floor. He kept thinking that: how nice it would have been to crumple slowly on to the floor. And pull his coat, over his head. Stop everything from happening.

I was just saying, said Esme, who seemed distracted, that you didn't really see what happened to Joe, did you? Apparently, he keeps waking up in the night in agony, the poor thing. But there's nothing wrong, as far as the doctors can see.

That sounds awful, poor thing.

He could feel the pressure of the cavity behind his eyes, bulging.

No, he continued, I didn't really see what happened. He didn't get hit though, did he? I mean, there wasn't a mark on him.

Michael sat dizzily.

Not a scratch, said Joe's mum. Doctors are calling it a – what? . . . a phantom pain. Reckon it's shock.

She sounded chipper enough, while her hand was twisting knots in and out of her necklace.

How are you, anyway, Mikey – your head and everything?

Uh?

Honestly, I wouldn't mind it myself. I could do with a good sleep.

Oh, said Michael, the coma. Yeah, I'm fine.

Esme kept glancing at him when Joe's mum wasn't looking – pointed, suspicious glances. A touch accusatory, maybe.

Fortnight in bed, thank you very much.

Sorry, I just have to—

He nodded out towards the garden in lieu of an excuse, began shuffling on his way.

Yeah, it'll be bedlam over there – I'd better get back.

She didn't stand.

He's – it's awful. He's in so much pain, there, and there's nothing—

She was clenching her nails into her palm, trying not to cry.

You just need to be able to do something, when they're yours, don't you? And—

A few teary throbs slipped out as Esme (glaring at her

husband) rubbed her back; she mutated them into a laugh.

It's daft really, isn't it? she said. All this worrying. They just get on with things, don't they?

Michael crept into the garden as innocuously as he could, trying not to think any more about his wife. It was getting dark. The security light barked at him.

He hid in the shed, listening to the sound of planes behind the cloud, aiming for the nearby airport. It soothed his nerves to imagine the smoke filling their cabins, their graceful fractures, the earth throwing up a curtain of dust the way a friend holds a coat around something you wouldn't want people to see. It felt almost like a penance, except for Esme's voice in his head: *Stop it, you're hurting people!*

Somebody was having a garden fire, smoke drifting across the fences. The smell returned him to Uncle Mike's impromptu bonfire on the front lawn (the reek of melting vinyl) and June, not long before they separated, trying to be calm, saying, *Be a good boy, hold Weldon for me*, while she banged on the front door: banging, trying to get his uncle to let her in, to turn down the music, to stop shouting. Telling him that the birds weren't conspiring against him. June banging on the door. The dog struggling back to his uncle, sensing he was in danger. Michael was angry with Weldon, scared of him; why couldn't he sit still, do as he was told, not make a scene? There was too much life cramped in that small dog – dragging him, half a step, towards the house. His uncle shouted from the window. The dog barked at the house. Michael dug in, pulled back; with Weldon's lead gripped in both hands, he learned the strain of love.

On the camping chair in the shed where he imagined his wife dying, his children dying, he thought of messaging his uncle Mike, see how he was. They were close when he was a kid, but then . . . he felt so far away, over the water. It all felt so far away. What would he even say? *How are things? I blinded someone today with my mind. Now I'm just trying not to imagine my wife falling out of love with me.* Not to do something so manipulative, so creepy. The moment he imagined Mara falling from the wall, he lost the right to fear the worst, to wallow in it – the comfort that comes from knowing you've already sunk a little way into the mud and seen the impression you'd leave behind.

He stared at the back of his house, working up the courage to make the few steps to his family.

Michael felt awkward at first, sitting in their bed. It felt like the scene of a crime. Esme was chewing her fingernail, staring at a book with an oil painting on the front, some long-dead woman in blue. He was struggling to distract himself with his phone.

That's sad, isn't it, about Joe.

Yeah, she said.

I mean, I wonder if I—

No, she interrupted him without glancing from her book. No.

Michael rubbed his temples. The scar tissue made one side more sensitive than the other; he didn't like to touch the vein that throbbed through the skin.

I think he senses it, Louis – that nothing bad's gonna happen.

Good, she said.

After the trip to the beach, Michael had put him to bed: *Are you OK, Louis? You can tell me if something's up.* He shrugged – part of the blithe indifference he'd grown, a belatedness, dawdling through the forest unbothered by the witch-screams from the oven, skirting around the fingers of the fallen giant, arriving in the ratless town to wonder, briefly, where all his mates were. As he lifted his lips from the forehead of his unresponsive son, Michael was pierced by a sudden fear: what would happen to his boy when he was gone?

But, he said (not daring to ask Esme to broach the future, to ask *What comes after us?*) . . . I dunno.

Whatever doesn't kill you makes you stronger, she said, rolling her eyes.

I never said that.

You were thinking it.

She turned away from him on to her side.

Did she know what he was thinking? Live with someone long enough and you get used to the idea that the skin's edge softens, that you begin to smudge into each other. But there is something final and separate about a body: the way it's lowered into a hole in the ground and melts into the lives of smaller things. There was an Esme that, even through the coma's amnesia, had survived in his mind. Unless he'd made it all up (ha!). The more he remembered of her, the more she hid from him. Retreating into her skin. Reading about things he couldn't understand, things that were no use talking to him about. Sometimes she'd stroll into a room and appear taken aback by the sight of him stirring a cup of tea or piecing one of his jigsaws – this unexpected man in her life, a *How-did-he-get-here?* kind of look. Surprising herself with marriage and children. She had, or seemed as though she had, exhausted herself of him: it took so much of her to bring him back here, you'd wonder if anyone could be worth such an expenditure of love.

⋆

Oh, what's up with Alex? he asked, as though he'd just remembered.

Nothing. She's fine.

But Joe's mum was—

From the jolt of her body, you'd think she'd just been shocked awake.

What are we doing here? she asked.

You what?

What the hell are we still doing here? Pretending to be a normal family? It's insane.

She sat up in bed.

But I thought you wanted—

It's completely insane. Living here, like we're some commuter-belt, semi-detached family. Why aren't we in Greece or, I dunno, yeah Greece?

We can go to Greece, if you want. Do you want to go on holiday to Greece?

No, it's just this! she gestured to the house. What the hell is this?

There was a dizzy moment where he saw them packing the car lightly, rushing to the airport and escaping. Then he realised he'd imagined them packing the car lightly, rushing to the airport and escaping. It wasn't impossible, it just felt impossible. He took her hand – she squirmed out of it. Stood outside the bed.

What about the kids, though? They're settled here.

She made an exasperated, grunting noise. Dropped her book.

This is insane. This is insane.

He opened his mouth, as if to say something – something like, *I think I've fucked up, Es.* Or even just, *I'm sorry.*

But it stopped in his chest. She sighed, sounding as though she'd given up.

They stared at each other. Until she left for the bathroom. Touching her head. Exasperated.

By the time she returned, he'd settled into a pretend sleep.

6

Midway in a meeting about an IT upgrade and Michael ought to have been in his element. Under the glow of spreadsheets and emails he'd already been semi-automated into a dull ghostliness. Mayonnaise Julian implicated him with an impassive smile at Rachel's repeated mentions of the new Incat case cataloguing system, his childish sense of humour delivered with a world-weary resignation. He knew he ought to have felt like he was really *one of the team* (again). But doodling a pair of eyes on the agenda that John had circulated, he felt instead an unease. Joe; the look the driver had given him; Esme, last night, standing in her pyjamas, looking robbed.

Ever since he reappeared from the coma, his amnesia had been slipping him new memories – odd little pieces of the jigsaw, the picture mutating with each piece. We all end unassembled. But, the driver that didn't hit Joe – it was as if she'd seen something final and unexpected. He remembered that morning in Esme's flatshare with Luc and the others, when he was trying to sneak out of her room back to his girlfriend without Lucas finding out (who would definitely tell, or at least leverage his guilt). Luc was coming back home from a night out and caught his friend at Esme's door, not unstupefied – as though he'd expected to encounter himself leaving her room and didn't quite recognise his own face. They nodded to each other; didn't say a word about it. Then, or ever.

It would have been better for his mental health if he could have suppressed all these memories of himself becoming a person, having emotions and acting on them, not acting on them (already he was nostalgic for the clean slate of his post-coma amnesia), but they returned sporadically, unbidden. Thinking of the future risked erasing it. He felt trapped in some mindfulness boot camp, having to exist continually *in the moment*. Only animals can bear the present tense for long; we live also outside of ourselves. Here was his past, haunting him incompetently. And here was their future, annihilated or unthinkable. So Michael grew riddled with shadows: the shadows of bricks, cancers, fires. He'd sit in the shed feeling sorry for himself, thinking you can make a fetish of pain and recovery, but what happens to someone if nothing ever goes wrong? Now, and now, came this interrogation: *What have you done?* Thinking of the kids, of Esme. *What have you done?* Thinking of Luc in a mind like his, of Luc and Esme, with suspicion, or jealousy. *What have you done?* He didn't know how to answer. But that didn't halt the interrogation. Out of nowhere: a vision of Julian's military eyes fixing him, seeing the moth-eaten inside of him, asking him to name the futures he'd erased, to take responsibility, staring at him, *What have you done?*

Julian, who yelled.

*

Or made a weird sort of quiet shriek, where a scream should have been – as though he'd exhaled every breath he'd ever taken in one short burst.

Well, the air had left the room. Jenny half-stood, and reached out a tender arm as she said

Julian—

What the—?

Oh my God!

There was a chair knocked on the floor.

Fucking hell.

Somebody ran out of the room, calling.

Angie! Angie!

Shit, Julian—

There were two sumps which were his eyes, his lids crinkling into them, and through the cracks you could glimpse a redness, throbbing.

Your eyes!

Has anyone phoned an ambulance?

If there'd been some blood to mop up it might have made things easier.

Sit down, Julian. Somebody get him a chair.

Here.

What can you see Julian? Can you see my hand? How many fingers?

Are you—? Jesus.

He looked small, surrounded by his colleagues, trying to see his fingers held up before him, through sore, eyeless skin.

I'll phone an ambulance, said Michael, trying to sound helpful – and not at all evasive, as he scuttled between desks. Half-tripped down the stairs. The vision of Julian's eyes; thinking, *This time you've done it.*

Out of the office. *This time you've ruined everything.*

To the car park.

Where the breeze was nudging the saplings as if it had just told a bad joke.

He felt all the usual things people feel when they've accidentally imagined someone's eyes away. Except that he also wanted to take up smoking again.

He'd have to go back.

He didn't go back.

She fixed things, she'd always fixed things. It was only when she answered that he regretted phoning Esme.

Hiya.

Hello, he tried to reply cheerily.

What's up?

He was crouched behind a Volkswagen estate in the office car park, peeking up through the windows to see if anyone was coming.

Oh, nothing much.

He put his fist in his mouth.

Well, what did you ring me at work for? I'm busy.

Just to say hello.

Hello.

He was desperate to scream *I'VE JUST VANISHED SOMEONE'S EYES.* Somehow it didn't seem like an appropriate thing to shout in the car park.

Oh, and do you fancy beef bourguignon for dinner, cos I'm going to head to the shop on the way home.

Did you mistake me for someone else?

(He'd remembered her enjoying his bourguignon on

their wedding anniversary, in spite of Louis' chickenpox, but – not now.)

Fair enough. I'll see you later then.

Are you OK?

Yeah!

OK, you just sound a bit . . .

. . .

Hhhmm, yeah. All right. Love you.

Love you too. Bye.

Bye-bye.

If anyone had been looking out of the window for the coming ambulance they would have seen Michael standing curiously behind a VW, slapping his head and talking to himself. Gulls were thudding across car bonnets. The sky scrolling from windscreen to windscreen.

He crept out from behind the car – he decided that he'd stand outside the office, pretend to be waiting to direct the paramedics. Except he wasn't really pretending. Blustered leaves flashed different shades. The office chaos breaking out in his mind. People with their heads in their hands. Running around with wet paper towels. Mishal standing, dazed, holding a stapler. Paul locking himself in the toilet. The crowd around Julian telling everyone to give him some space, to let him breathe. John making sensible suggestions about first aid. Sam wheezing on her hands and knees, crawling beneath the tables for his eyes.

He was shaking involuntarily. Maybe he shouldn't have come outside without his coat. With his hand at his mouth, he decided to give it a go: he imagined Julian with no eyes.

He'll be fine, he said. It'll be fine.

Trees, cars, sky; he felt guilty about the light falling into his eyes, the world that it rebounded to him. He closed them.

Smothered under his hands, the light echoed in his eyes.

Sirens approached, sounding fearful. The air smelled of petrol and coming rain. Paramedics dropped from the ambulance; he couldn't make eye contact with them – watched his shadow lift its hand to its mouth and imagined it was smoking a cigarette, the summer sky of its nicotine moving into him.

When Michael walked back into the office, barely a head lifted. They were all typing away, on the phones, consulting each other about tricky cases. It was as if he'd just been for a cigarette break. Then they saw the paramedics and curiosity struck.

Warily, he led them to Julian, who was back at his desk, staring nowhere through a pair of dark glasses. Nobody in the office seemed shocked, just confused by the presence of the paramedics.

Here, he said, pointing to Julian's eyes.

One of the paramedics touched the other on the shoulder.

There was a perplexed, slightly disdainful look on the office's faces. Jenny strode over to Michael and led him away while Lucy spoke to the paramedics.

What the hell Michael?

I—

Is this supposed to be funny?

But, his eyes.

Jesus Christ, we're not at school any more. Prank-calling paramedics? Are you out of your mind?

Sorry, I – I'd forgotten.

How could—

She paused; the certainty of what she was about to say dissipated. Her whole body seemed to sink, as though she couldn't remember how long Julian had been that way (something to do with the war maybe?), half-recalling some chaos in the office that could just have been a scene from TV. She shivered and looked back at Michael.

Look, I know this hasn't been easy for you, and if I'm completely honest I thought it might all have been too soon.

She sighed.

You grab your things and go home. I'll sort this out. We'll pretend it never happened.

Michael stood awkwardly by the printer; it wanted nothing to do with him. She was already charming the paramedics. He smiled as though he was wearing somebody else's face.

How large the desire to be small and hidden from the world when things go awry. So Michael went in search of somewhere to be unseen. For reasons he couldn't quite explain, he locked himself in the car. As though its windows were less than transparent (they weren't). But at least the car park was a non-place: a hiatus, edged by reeds and grasses growing up to the motorway. Being there felt like an intermission.

He'd erased Julian's eyes. Everybody had seen the empty sockets. He had imagined the chaos in the office. Now it was like nothing had happened. Except, it felt tacit. Suppressed maybe. Everybody knew. They must have known, somewhere under the clay of their thoughts. And carried on regardless. Maybe they didn't believe themselves. Maybe, frustrating the aftermath, it became the lie they had in common. Too dangerous to say: to speak is to risk denial. But they'd be out soon. They'd see him in the car. And maybe—

Shivering, he clicked the seatbelt automatically. The clasp tutted. He reversed out of the bay, into the world.

Next, like a child in a fairy tale, he hid in the woods, where surprises live. Pacing its lanes, its clearings, trying to empty his head. But walking's problem is that it's thinking masquerading as movement.

Jenny's hand kept revisiting his shoulder. *I know this hasn't been easy for you.* The confused, awkward silence in the office. *I know this hasn't been easy for you.* Julian, glaring uselessly at him through dark glasses.

He almost wanted to run home, to look at his mum with that face reserved for a parent, the one that says *I've done something really bad*, and comes to them to be the person who mends, who understands the world. They brought you through so much worse, the near-death of a birth – they can get you through this. As a kid he'd crawl beneath the coats in the cupboard, half-hoping that if he could just sit it out for long enough, when he stepped out of the door and into the forest, a blizzard would have cancelled everything, and there'd only be the sound of his footsteps creaking, the branches drowsy with snow.

★

But there was no snow. Just muck and mulch. Things' decay. (That blind face.) The stuff that clings to your dog, there in your mind, as you try to imagine him not existing, again. Pacing. Again. There being no dog. And it not working, again.

The drive home was quiet, the sound of the engine ruminating. A lowering sun pulled the shadows out from under things like a cheap magician. Michael could feel everyone's eyes on him – a tacky kind of guilt. It was unravelling so quickly – but if he could concentrate, he could fix things. If he could— (Those dark glasses, staring at him – was that undoing it? It didn't feel undone.) The influenza of remorse creeping its ache into his musculature.

He sat in the car outside his house for a while, letting the migraine bore in behind his eye. Wondering, in the pallid light of his mind, what he was going to tell Esme. He watched the pigeons sidling in stop motion across the roof as though they daren't come down.

He went inside. Said nothing.

With her head bowed into the blueish light, he watched her, eating her boiled egg.

The fever of guilt seizing his neck, his back. Imagining the police officers at the door. *Is Michael there?* With a measured whack, he did for the top of his second egg. *We'd like to ask you some questions.* It looked sutured, but with a second crack it split, the yolk looked up, perfect. *Your colleague, Julian Hicks, why did you blind him?* He couldn't eat it, at first.

5

By the time he woke the next day, the walls were sweating. His skin so sensitive even the sound of a delivery van could bruise it. He remembered Esme leaving somewhere in his fevered sleep, her goodbye kiss lifting from his forehead like a moth. She'd dropped the kids off and gone to work, having left honey and lemonade (now tepid) by his bedside table, various tablets and a note asking him to imagine them with Ebola, coronavirus, bird flu and bubonic plague. Again.

The light sinking through the curtains was sore. Michael wrapped himself up in the duvet. It felt as though the hair on his skin was crawling elsewhere. A pressure bulged between his vertebrae. Prising his shoulder blades. Pressing at the occipital bone from deep within his skull. The kind of pressure that made him want to crack a hole in his body and let it all splurge through. He couldn't stop it: the memory of those dark glasses, eyeballing him.

Michael stalked Julian online. All the photos of him with the Forces lot. Smiles clinging on to their faces. If pushed (or drunk), he sang 'Superstition' (not terribly) at the karaoke down the Crown and Bucket. He ran the marathon in a rhino costume. And then again in memory of Imogen. Michael wished there was a social-media platform where people confessed how awful they were, for either of their sakes. (There almost certainly was. He wasn't prepared for it.)

Obviously, he imagined himself with a migraine. It only seemed to make things worse.

At some point, he managed to limp to the bathroom. It was too white, too bright in there. The odd golf ball arcing over the treetops. He stayed on the toilet for a while, waiting for his dead leg to return, imagining the hazmat suits emerging from a Nissan Micra to carry him away.

The voices on the other side of the wall were laughing at something. Was that what woke him up? He'd been in the middle of some dream, walking through the town while Julian kept pointing at Mara, saying *She was about her size.* Through the wall an old sitcom was repeating; every now and then his neighbours joined in, but most of the laughter was canned.

In quieter moments there came a knocking (was someone mending a fence?). He kept thinking about Julian: feeling his way through the world, having only a yard of future ahead of him, imagined from the dark tap of a white stick.

Aching above sleep, he had a vision of the town as the blackbird sees it, hidden in the treetop: so vivid, so vertiginous, he was careful not to move an inch from the edge of the bed in case he fell fifteen feet to the ground; the whole place going about its business, oblivious. Only the blackbird had a nail in its skull.

It was dark and Alex's voice (which was almost Esme's voice, only with the surprise and hesitation of not being in her sister's body) was nudging the kids through their dinner downstairs. *Why wasn't she Esme?* he thought. She must have been at work, or something – Alex looking after the kids. He staggered down to see them.

I'm eating dinosaurs! shouted Mara.

Louis was more circumspect.

Wow, said Alex. Are you all right? Can I get you anything?

A spade might do, said Michael, leaning his head against the fridge.

No offence, but you look worse than when you were in the coma.

Where's Esme?

Oh, she had something urgent on at work or something. I didn't mind – nice to get out of the city for a day, see these two terrors! Are you sure I can't get you anything?

Your sister, he thought. He took two cheese slices back upstairs after grinning monstrously at the children.

★

The cheese slices were deliciously cool;

(He remembered – had he just thrown a strop? – his mum resting cucumber slices on his eyes, *You'll like this*; their coolness lifting the heat of his overcharged brain.)

but by the time Alex was reading to Mara – the odd word, *enormous . . . space . . . cliff . . . nothingness* clarifying through the walls – he had two sweaty cheese squares covering his eyes.

In a daze, he tried to imagine them with plagues and infections, but his mind kept drifting to the inquest when they found out about Julian – the people coming out of their houses, hounding him into the town with prods from golf clubs and selfie sticks, the butcher holding a string of sausages menacingly. Then the trial on the green by the yew tree, Julian's weird eyes staring at him as though he'd seen all this before and was no longer surprised, Uncle Mike already hung from the tree, a look on his face as if to say, *yup.* The reflection of his unlaced trainers dangling on the blackeye of the pond.

A screech: car wheels, daylight. He'd dreamed he'd been walking along a desolate road on his way to a DIY shop when a van came from nowhere and was about to hit him.

The light chiselled into his head. (He remembered waking with a lancing hangover in Esme's room, without Esme – them not long together. That print over her bed of some Renaissance painting: the sickly woman on the floor with a slack wrist and a nick at the throat, the bloke crouched over her wearing furry trousers and the haircut of a nineties Italian footballer. What was the dog doing there?) There was tepid water at his bedside. Some commotion outside. He drank. He slept.

Esme's voice was downstairs. Her work clothes bunched on the dresser; dematerialised into the knuckles and creaks of the house, her movements below him, from room to room, crackling in and out of space. He was desperate for her to come up to talk to him and had no idea what to say.

Sweating into the duvet, he could hear her muffled voice, her sister's. Alex was crying. *I'm so sorry – I thought he was playing with his friends . . .* Something about Louis, *lying down on the road . . .* The screech . . . *Said he wanted to see what would happen . . .* He should've got up – that screech, he should have known it was his son . . . *scared to tell Michael . . .* He crawled out of bed. Over to Louis' room. The boy was asleep. His only real privacy, the only world he had completely apart from his parents, his auntie, his teachers, his friends. And unless Michael woke him mid-dream, to tell him he loved him, to tell him that he was here for him, that bereaved world would vanish, unremembered. *I'm so sorry, Es . . .* Her voice being squeezed by Esme . . . laughing (sobbing), *It's probably for the best, my hostile womb . . .* Michael crept back into bed. *It'll happen.*

And it's not like you'd be any worse than Mum . . . Pulled the covers over his head. Their muffled voices hugging each other. *Remember when she left us on the train?* Laughter that was theirs, that only came out for each other. He found it hard, sometimes, to tell their voices apart. Which one of them was saying, *You have an idea of the life you want, and then it's compromise after compromise . . .* He rolled over. *Depends on who you're compromising for.*

Later, Alex left. Esme didn't come up.

Esme?

Something awoke him, alone in bed. With the screw drilled deep into his eye, the sweat dried into a paste on his neck, he grappled himself downstairs for a glass of water. Esme was asleep in front of the TV, watching horse trials live from the daylit side of the world through her eyelids. There was a moment when he was confused about why it was dark outside, but the horses were jumping novelty fences with the sun's gloss on their hide. (He remembered when he shifted hemispheres for that fortnight to visit Gaz; Esme said it was as though his daylight was the light of her dreams. When he came home, jetlagged and wrapped in night, she sat up from bed, rubbing her eyes, as though she was expecting someone else.)

He pulled the blanket over his wife – kissed her, trying not to wake her with the stench of his breath.

4

Daylight wasn't so sore; reddening softly and already it was too late. He'd slept the whole day through. The house felt empty. Michael had shrivelled. But he managed the stairs. Hungrily ate a turkey and pesto sandwich. Alex had left a note about dropping the kids at his parents, something illegible about Esme and archives. Esme – he saw her sinking into their room last night, sitting on the edge of the bed. *I'm not sure about you*, she said in a low voice. But he'd spent the mess of the last few days lapsing in and out of intense dreams. Tasted things in them, touched things. Seen weirdnesses in daylight. There she was, or wasn't, despondent on the edge of the bed, shoving him lightly to make sure he was awake, or wasn't, saying *I'm not sure about you*.

He was alone with the television. Trying not to worry about Esme, to wonder too much about her. Through the residue of his headache, he watched documentaries about food production, drug dealers, that kind of thing. Eventually, through it all, with his head on the plump sofa cushion, he fell back to sleep.

Finally. He woke to the sound of her key slurring in the door. A three-point-turning car. Things dropped from her – keys, bag, coat – on the way to the kitchen, where she guzzled from a carton of orange juice.

What? she said, wiping her mouth.

(*What's the deal with you and Es?* It came to him, staring at the cheap wood of the table. The pub wreathed with familiar voices, the way the chairs tilted on that anaemic red carpet, the crisp packet unseamed between them, and Luc probing, trying to uncover how someone like Esme wound up with someone like Michael rather than, say, someone like him.)

He followed the sound to the kitchen.

Where've you been?

He tried not to sound accusatory.

You hadn't pictured me being fished out from the river, had you?

He shrugged, dismissively. Her features were drifting apart from each other, drunk.

I've been at the museum, she laughed, where else?

I'm not bothered where you go, Esme. But you could

at least tell me. My head's in pieces. The last thing I need is worrying where you are.

I think we both know you have nothing to worry about.

She drunkenly scooped crispfuls of hummus into her mouth.

What, don't you believe me? I've been having a party with the statues.

(This was hilarious.)

Do you want some crisps?

I'm fine, thanks.

He yawned up on to his feet.

Ssshhhhh, shhhh! she whispered. The kids are in bed!

They're at Mum's. But I'm going up.

No! Don't go! We're having a crisps and hummus party.

(When they were arguing over leaving the city, she threw her mojito down the drain and shouted in front of everyone enjoying their falafel and hummus wraps at the street food market, *I feel like a fucking teenager here!* He wanted to say, *I feel like a teenager there!* – he'd spied her scouting places near his mum and dad. Instead, he looked at her, lamb-eyed, and kind-of-truthfully said, *Is this about me getting mugged?*)

I'm tired Esme. My head's sore. I'm going to bed.

She threw a crisp at him.

You're no fun since the coma. You've become an old man.

He remembered her repeating it, *I feel like a fucking teenager.* They'd move out into their age, into the hopefulness of kids and kids. Kids would correct everything. The city felt so close to the creeping disaster – its air, its protests. From up on the hills you could still almost see it, smoking towards them. But out here, they could pretend none of it was happening. Could live the future that belonged to older people, just about.

And now – he thought, *Now – I'll do it.*

Wait there, he said, pulling open drawers and cupboards. Rummaging for – for what? Anything that would do. An elastic band? A keyring? Not a Hula Hoop. The panic was beginning to set in – this was taking him too long. (Esme had stopped asking what he was doing and started to look bored.) Anything – to confirm them, to confirm everything. Them: a family, reborn from crisis. Untouchable. He grabbed a can of Coke Zero from the fridge. Sucked the froth from his fidgety opening. Ripped the ring pull. Found himself on one knee, in front of Esme, trying not to hurt his finger on the sharp edge.

Esme, he said.

She had her hand over her mouth.

I know this isn't perfect, but—

What was he going to say? He'd prepared for this. It was useless. Something – *I can keep us safe if you can bring us to life.* No, that was awful. Something like: *I can't imagine a future without you* – no, *I can imagine a future without you.* That was right, wasn't it? It didn't sound right, but they loved each other and he knew he should just say what he felt and everything would be fine and—

Fuck, right, off, she said, on the verge of laughing. Just fuck off, she said correcting herself with incredulity, wafting him away.

Wafting all of this away. She (mis)stepped from the kitchen towards the stairs.

Jesus – fucking, Coke Zero, she mumbled. Why the hell did I bother coming back here?

*

While she was in the bathroom he slipped into bed. Going over it. His long balance of corrections and incorrections, the mess of living with people, that all he wanted was the quiet, simple hospital bed, the economy of its white sheet, its black mind. With the duvet pulled up to his chin, going over it: *I feel like a fucking teenager.* Catching the train out to view the newbuilds by his parents' house. The nostalgic hopefulness of the old pubs, with their beer gardens, their new leaves pushing out from the branches, as though this thing had been going on for centuries. Arguing with her on the train, because it felt inevitable that she'd get bored of him – especially out here, where the ground dampens around your ankles and the ivy has its hand on your shoulder. Out here, where even people's dogs know who you are. She'd find out all about him out here, how tedious he was, how boring, how nothing he was, and leave him. So he prodded. *We're still young! What d'you want to live like my parents for?* Out here, where art is oil paintings of classic cars and music is the busker outside the shoe shop doing 'Red Red Wine'. Out here, with its quiet fold of hills to tuck you in, with its grass growing over your head. *I feel like a fucking teenager*, she'd said.

3

In the freezer aisle Michael faced up to his consequences. But only after that night had passed slowly, lying beside Esme's clumsy breathing, turning back and back again over blinding a man, little Joe who was hurting all over and didn't know what hadn't happened to him, his kids, his wife. Luc. The ring pull from a can of Coke Zero. Everything breaking apart. He wanted to run outside and kick a dog or something (not really), do a window in, spray-paint how unfair it all is over the parish hall. It'd mean admitting what he'd done, and although he knew that coming clean was always an unburdening, he couldn't. The liar's relief is being able to step from the fantasy world they're constantly assembling and reassembling into the same world as everyone else. That wouldn't be him: his confession couldn't readmit him to the world of other people, it didn't belong. Michael didn't go outside and smash a window or kick a dog. He lay beside his sputtering wife, trying, mid-ocean, to piece together the wrecked boat of his family, from driftwood and foam.

In the schema of marriage-saving-gestures, i.e. holidays in St Lucia, expensive jewellery or radical surgery, his plan of a couple's trip to the out-of-town supermarket would be commended for originality.

We're going to an exhibition! he said in the car park, trying to cover over the night before with ebullience. It's all about culture's victory over nature.

She didn't smile.

He was determined to prove to Esme that they could recover their normal selves, in much the same way the un-comatose learn to speak or use cups again. (Not him, of course, he just feared he'd never be able to and drank his tea like nothing had ever happened.) His wife had a wraith of a hangover and lingered in the cooler reaches of the refrigerated sections. Her husband had come with the idea of restocking themselves, but the way she dumped things in the trolley was more suggestive of a visit to the tip. She barely spoke. Almost-non-committal *uhs* and head-lolls as comments on whatever he was holding up. She seemed finally bored. In lieu of affection, they had mute disagreements about washing detergent. By the time they'd reached the tinned goods, he realised he'd made a mistake. That he should have nursed her hangover at home, sunk to its level, returned the favour for her coma vigils. Left the kids at his mum's and curled up on the sofa. Instead, they were here, between the milk and the yoghurt, at the end of the world.

He sighed, or the trolley wheel – one of them sighed.

It was a decent effort, he said to himself, as though he'd spooned a shot almost to the corner flag. He gave up on dragging Esme back to the normality he remembered and set off to finish the shopping. Left her to cant from aisle to aisle, gawking at the shelves until they made sense.

*

Michael felt the buzz of his phone again. That dull, intrusive buzz that found him fantasising about throwing it in a ditch and scarpering from field to field across fences. Luc kept calling, sending messages. He wasn't in the mood to face him. Was talking to himself instead, dull on the frost-touched window, trying to find something frozen that the kids wouldn't complain about.

Fish fingers . . . fish fingers . . . fish fingers . . .

A whack at his ankle. Michael presumed someone had clipped him with their trolley and turned for an apology. Julian. Smiling towards the space where Michael's face just about was. He had his sister on one arm. His stick tucked in at the elbow of the other.

I thought I heard you! he said.

Michael smiled uneasily. Imagined the plain-clothes officers grabbing his hands from behind . . .

You remember Michael, don't you? Julian lifted his face towards his sister. In my year. Used to hang out with that weird kid, Lucas.

Long time ago, she said, shaking her head and laughing politely.

. . . marching him out of the shop with a bag over his head to stop him picturing them . . .

Colleagues now.

Nice to meet you, she said. Then mumbled something into Julian's ear about being back in a minute, departing with the shopping list.

★

. . . driving him to a white, bright room, where he'd been scanned and prodded until it was all unravelled . . .

How you doing, anyway? Feels like you've been off forever.

. . . and they left him in a quiet room, puddling in guilt; because he had blinded this man. Because Michael was looking at a man who wouldn't see the rest of his life happening to him. Because he'd done it, and couldn't undo it.

Oh, you know, he said. Back next week, hopefully.

Head again?

Yeah. Anyway, hope you're well – I just need to catch up with my wife, she's—

I was thinking about you the other day, Julian interrupted.

Oh yeah.

Esme was drifting back towards them; Michael wriggling for an escape.

We—

The coma – maybe . . . Right now I'm miles from everything, you know? Stuff just comes at me from, like, nowhere. But, I swear it wasn't always like this.

Esme was back by the trolley; she smiled at Julian, then realised what the glasses and stick signified, but didn't say anything.

Except, no one can remember me going blind. It's driving my sister mad. Some of the Four-Two lads reckoned it was when our Jackal got rolled – but I can see myself coming home, you know what I mean?

He was tapping his head with a finger.

That's so strange, said Michael, trying not to sound distracted.

He touched Esme's back; she was unresponsive.

Christ, I can see myself in the office with you! And I've tested it, like – *describe this, describe that* – I've seen it, you know. I get it right. I can see it all in my head. I just feel . . . I dunno . . . I feel, there's a gap, you know?

Michael puffed air through his lips, made a surprised face. Then realigned to Julian's blindness.

That's really weird.

Is that what it was like for you? With the coma?

I mean, sort of, yeah. But—

Like something's missing? Not just something you had, but your future and all? It's – I dunno, I feel like I've been banished, you know?

Esme began to walk away. That stunned, soft-toed walk where you don't want to touch anything else in case it moves. Michael motioned to go after her, but Julian half-stepped in the way. Neither mentioned it.

But I'm right here. I mean, the coma – I know it's not the same, but, no offence, you were a bit weird after, like you were missing something?

I—

Esme was past the end of the aisle.

Something tells me you'd understand, you know?

I'm sorry, mate, said Michael. I don't think I understand.

He tried to think of something else, something more convincing to say.

If there's anything I can do – anything to help you . . .

Julian shrugged, numb to it. It's not your problem.

★

Michael had squirmed past him, mumbling something about seeing him at work. Past the aisle, through the checkout lines. Esme was gone.

She didn't answer her phone. He scanned dumbly around the supermarket, the way you look for a lost child.

The aisles.

The checkouts.

Julian strafing his stick up the aisle towards his sister's voice, striking chinks of light from the dark.

There'd been an empty bay where their car was supposed to be. Michael had set off on foot. Oblivious to the changes to the landscape near his home – the clearances, the cutbacks, as though the council had swept through with a fleet of hedge-trimmers and bulldozers.

Arriving with a thin clag of sweat and shopping-bag aches stretched into his arms (well he wasn't just going to leave a half-full trolley ghosting the aisles, was he?), Michael found his parents agitating the front of his house. Mum, ear to the door. Dad, peering in at the window. The kids—

Esme picked them up, his mum said, with a saintly hand concerning her chest, a *where've you been?* look on her face.

Of course, he said, pretending he'd misremembered plans. The vision was there before he could stop it: speeding home from the supermarket, urgent packing, then round to his parents to bundle the kids into the car, Esme turning to the back seats with an edgy ebullience, *We're going on an adventure!* It crawled on him, feeling devious, furtive. Even being in the house was wrong: how knowing a rat is hidden in the garden makes everything creep.

They smiled, pretending they'd just popped in on their Saturday morning walk.

Cup of tea? Coffee?

Trying again to be normal.

While the kettle boiled, he tried phoning Esme. The dial tone. The rumbling water. No answer.

The shopping gave him an excuse to leave them in the living room with a cup of coffee while he put things away. Gave him a chance to set his story straight.

He didn't manage to set his story straight. Edgy on his peripheries, half-expecting Julian and his dark glasses to appear.

Coffee was the quietness of unsaid things: his mum desperate to ask what was going on with him and Esme, but too far into a life conditioned against prying. His dad stared out of the window as though he was standing at the end of a pier. The sound of Julian's stick tapping in Michael's mind, its metronomic guilt.

Are you feeling better now, then? I phoned the other day, but Alex said you were having a lie-down. I said I thought you'd be sick of lying down, after everything lately. She laughed. I thought it was Esme at first – her voice. It wasn't.

Michael nodded. Offered no further explanation.

This was how it went when they visited his uncle in his flat. The one on what his mum called the *restitution estate*, as though he'd been taken from himself. She must have liked the word 'rest' in there. That was her refrain, *More rest.* (*Nothing is at absolute rest* Michael remembered copying into his workbook from the whiteboard.) His uncle just seemed bored – which was easy to sympathise with. The three of them there, lengthening his hours: you could feel the agitation in all that stillness. The forest's electrons in his second-hand furniture. Mites competing beneath his bed in the dust-warrened dark. How near they were to his private anxieties. For the love of God, he just wanted them to leave him to himself.

I'm worried about the kids.

His mum had burst into words, as though she'd been trying to keep it under the surface. His dad laid an admonishing hand on her arm, gave her the *We talked about this* face of a long, intuitive marriage. Her glance back at him: *I know, but we have to say something.* His exhale: *Fine, on your head be it.*

They're—

Michael squinted at her.

Well, Louis – he barely moves. It's like he's got ME or something. And Mara, she's in a world of her own. Talking to herself and – nothing's real with her. She barely notices we're there.

They're fine.

He swallowed, knowing that they're not fine. That the gap in the world he was leaving for them was shrinking. He was closing them in. Maybe they should escape. The cemetery trees, garden blooms, ivy walls: everything here was pulled apart by roots. The comfort of coming back, when everything else felt so vertiginous – to pull the green blanket of the (almost) countryside over you, and go to sleep; him, here, this, it was smothering them. Uncle Mike did right, cleared off elsewhere. Was that what he was instilling in him, when he was a kid? Always taking him to the beach, staring at the sea with those long, grey thoughts becoming emptiness.

I don't want to pry, Michael, you know I don't want to pry, but—

How's Uncle Mike getting on? he asked, to change the conversation.

His mum looked to his dad, horrified.

That sheer, ice-sheet collapse of a look: he remembered everything. The weird months after, Mum going into a sort of dazed hibernation, nobody ever telling him what had actually happened until that night years later; his dad touching his thinning hair defensively, looking cautiously up to the ceiling where his wife was sleeping – when he'd asked *what happened* to Uncle Mike: the spacious Midtown apartment, the loving widow, the invalidated life-insurance policy. It had been unmentionable for years, but that night his dad's glass was cobwebbed with froth. *He landed on the pavement* (was Dad smiling when he said this?) *like a beached shark.* From only the sixth floor, it turned out. Of course, it wasn't a pavement, it was a sidewalk. Michael Dubbele, who worked on the fifth floor and was apparently the last person to see him alive, said Uncle Mike – falling to his death – looked annoyed at himself. Not suicidal; more as if he'd made a really dumb mistake, like dropping a bowl of cereal on to the floor out of curiosity.

I've just had a long morning. I—

His mum, red-eyed, mouth opening and closing in search of words, kept looking at him as she walked to the front door. His dad, with one arm around her shoulder, patted him with the other as they passed.

I— I'll call later, he said pathetically.

His memories of his uncle still felt as though they belonged to a living space. Five minutes earlier, Uncle Mike could've walked through the door with no bulge in the surface of Michael's reality. And now.

He hugged his startled mum before they left. She was too stunned to hug back. After a few steps, his dad turned back with a hesitant wave, his white hair sublimating into the pale-gold light.

Esme still wasn't answering her phone. He had to leave the house. He was trespassing there: it was too homely, too human. And so full of endings – he could feel the slow tidal wave of earth coming to make landfill of it all.

He avoided the town and the woods, headed through the railway underpass to the stony lanes, the brown ridged fields waiting to rise up in green uniformity. His uncle moving through his mind (it felt indulgent to repeat a grief for a man whose funeral he'd attended half his life ago); the pair of them sanding his piano, painting it, dripping eggshell-blue on the dust covers over the sofa, on the bare floorboards. Even an hour ago, those long-fingered hands were as alive in the flesh as they were in his memory. Maybe that's what Julian meant by *missing* – that although he knew he was blind, a part of him refused to believe he couldn't see. How Michael kept hearing a tapping stick, but never turned around because he knew, or thought he knew, there was never anything really there.

*

It had been so long since he'd walked this way, except in memories; the place was unrecognisable. Most of the barns around these parts had either been converted or had gone completely. Had he done this? Here, the town – he'd been so delirious with the migraine that he didn't know what he'd imagined, so amnesiac from the coma that he didn't know what he'd misremembered. Nothing was growing – not even wild flowers or tough grass. The irrigation ditch at the edge of the lane was a black gouge of dirt, drying out. Willow leaves shivered in windlessness, light tilting through the tree from leaf to leaf, from nowhere and into nothing.

Luc was right about the place, the way it weeds into you. Right to have left. Michael thought his mate had rid himself of it. Which was why the sight of him standing at the fence up ahead looked so out of place. There were scuffs of mud on his shoes, the hem of his suit, and the look on his face was of a map upside down.

All right, mate!

Michael tried to seem like he hadn't been ignoring his messages, his calls. Luc stared at him coming up the lane, took a rough swig of his beer.

What's up?

Luc pointed to the field. Stony earth. A foundation of scored and pitted concrete. A few trees, amputated, as though they'd outgrown their welcome.

I can't find my cows.

Michael's nervous smile wasn't reciprocated; Luc squinted at his approach.

I don't think they sell cows on the derivatives market, mate.

Luc didn't laugh. Looking down, he seemed a little surprised to find himself in a suit and wholly unsuitable shoes.

I left a herd of cows right here, and now they've fucked off.

Michael chuckled, but soon stopped.

Have you tried looking two decades ago?

For a moment Luc grinned.

Two decades ago, yeah.

Then he downed the last of his beer – dropped the can. Stamped on it. And launched it as far as he could into the field.

Milky fuckers!

Michael had to suppress a snigger; he couldn't tell if Luc was joking or drunk or weird. The numbness of it all left him feeling disembodied, everything unravelling so close and so far beyond him.

You've been here – where the fuck's it all gone?

Did no one buy it after it was, you know? said Michael, trying not to think that he'd vanished it. I thought they were gonna build houses, weren't they?

Lucas vaulted the fence clumsily, began kicking at the dirt, picking things out of it – stones, flint, litter – and tossing them away, dissatisfied. Kicking at the rotten stumps that marked the boundary.

Where's my fucking childhood gone?

Michael wanted to say something soothing about it being sold or repossessed, torn down or blown away. Something that was true. Or would at least sound truer than *I may have accidentally imagined it out of existence.*

Mate! Michael leaned his neck over the fence. Luc! Do you wanna come to my house for some beers? Or go to the pub?

⋆

Dust scuffs, the scuttling of stones, odd bits of rusted metal that Luc would investigate, throw away; Michael had given up trying to tease his friend back over the fence and just leaned on the gate, watching him off in his own little world. It felt familiar. The days spent with Luc in the woods, trying to coax him back to play footy while he carved faces into the trees for target practice with his BB gun.

Climbing over to join him would have meant conceding, so he waited until Luc came dawdling back, struggling to clear the fence.

They drifted towards the train station, not at any real pace. Luc kept insisting that he needed to get home, almost reminding himself that he had a job in the city that he should be at. (What day was it? Michael's last day in the office was his last undisorientated day.) Luc eventually offered his old friend one of the beers he'd brought with him; it was warm, but at least it was expensive. Michael knew he had to get back to Esme – hopefully – but felt a fragility in his friend that he didn't want to leave alone with these hacked-back trees, these birdless trees, the sound of small things hiding at their passing footsteps. They tried talking about football, as though they were fourteen again, Esme's voice in the back of his mind: *It's later than you think.*

Yeah, but he doesn't play football, said Luc with a weird intensity, he fucking wreaks it.

I can erase things by thinking about them.

It's like he's got a vendetta against – you what?

Ever since the coma. Bricks. Car crashes. All sorts of things happening to the kids.

Luc laughed.

Does Esme get an allowance for looking after you?

I'm not joking, mate, said Michael earnestly. I think I've fucked up.

Honestly don't know how she does it.

Aren't you listening? I can vanish stuff by thinking about it. Stop things happening.

Vanish stuff, yeah . . .

Michael faced him pathetically, like they were eleven again and all he needed in the world was for Luc to agree that his best mate really had seen something, UFO or not.

Remember when you said you were gonna take the school computers down with your hacking skills? said Luc. You had a floppy disc in the front of your bag with WORM written on it.

Look – look at that fencepost –

Not even a fucking CD. A floppy fucking disc.

I'm gonna vanish it.

Lucas didn't seem interested.

The damp-chewed post, leaning at an old man's angle went – its draggle of wire drooping to the earth.

There! Gone!

You thought you were in – shit, what was it called? That hacking film? Where they hack the military?

Look – it's gone, the fencepost – I vanished it!

What? There was never anything there.

There was!

Carry on vanishing things, said Luc sarcastically, and the only thing left will be God.

It was – I just vanished it.

Fuck me – listen to yourself. This is worrying, this, mate. Have you spoken to someone?

I'm telling you now!

I meant someone medical.

I think it's a bit beyond that.

Their childhood was him trying to impress Luc. Jump the gap. Throw the brick. Eat the spider. It was impossible: Michael was ruled by his dinnertime, bathtime, bedtime. There he was, burrowed up in himself like a hedgehog while Luc, fluctuant and wilful, trespassed across the fields and lock-ups and fences like a fox.

You should see someone, mate. Look at what happened to your uncle.

Stand still –

Michael grabbed Luc's arm.

stand still.

His shoes: mud-scutted brogues, the grey scuffs where he'd been kicking stones, the damp tips of the splayed laces: gone.

There!

What?

Your shoes!

What about them?

They're gone. I vanished your shoes.

Why the fuck would you do that? You don't go around vanishing people's shoes. I—

Luc looked down at his feet, puzzled. Momentarily.

I— I wasn't wearing any shoes.

You were! Why wouldn't you be wearing shoes?

He considered his damp socks, lifted his left foot, the sole already prickling with small stones.

It's good for you – there's lots of research into it. Health benefits . . .

Come on – think about it, you were here, in your shoes. Why would you be out here without your shoes?

Why would I be back here at all?

For Esme.

(Michael surprised himself; it just came blurting out.)

Who?

Esme.

There was barely any wind in the dry branches. Far off, the road's tide. A nearby bird was squeaking unreal, dog-toy squeaks.

Esme, Esme?

Michael nodded.

What the fuck are you on about?

He shrugged.

Esme.

Luc rested his hand on Michael's shoulder, settled, gave him a long, serious look. Then burped.

I'm being serious, Luc. She loves you, doesn't she?

He was laughing, tripping a little, up the lane, wincing on the edges of his feet.

Well?

Oh what, are you telling me women like Esme aren't what they seem? Luc grinned.

Do you remember the night we got together, me and Esme, and you saw me coming out of her room, what were you thinking?

I don't remember.

Roughly?

How the fuck should I know? Why don't you imagine it.

He shoved Michael, hard, chuckling as though it was playful. Gripped the back of his neck.

Think, said Michael, resisting the urge to push him back.

Oh, fuck off. It was half a fucking life ago! I dunno. I was probably thinking you're a paranoid dickhead in excellent trainers.

Michael thought for a second about offering his shoes, but –

She does, doesn't she. You and her.

Luc turned on him, grabbed him by the throat, held him (just about) up against the hedgerow.

What's the matter with you? Can't you see how much she loves you?

The dry thatch of it was digging into his back, scratching his face.

You've got what you wanted, mate. Your safe little life. Your fucking marriage. Your kids.

The brittle arms of the hedge collapsing around him, catching his skin; Michael felt as though he was falling through to the other side of it.

Bollocks. You love Esme.

Are you a fucking simpleton? Grow up.

He shoved Michael loose, who stumbled a few steps – touched the side of his face, checked the back of his hands, covered in scratches. The pair of them doing battle like flimsy teenagers.

Well why are you so angry then? Eh?

Luc opened his mouth, as though he was going to have the last word – an insult, or apology; Michael couldn't tell.

He looked like he was about to cry. Luc shook his head wearily and turned away, walking down the lane.

Brushing the clinging twigs from his jacket, Michael watched his mate hook up the half-spilled can from the floor, stumble away. He felt stupid, with his schoolboy jealousy; beside the point.

Luc! he shouted.

Luc didn't turn round.

Shadows sulked out from the hedgerows, crepuscular (how did it get so late?) and fluttering off homeward: the landscape of Michael's dinnertime, when the midges were out battling, and there was a haunted silo for the pair of them to investigate, or they still hadn't wreaked their vengeance on the man who caught them trying to pilfer football stickers from the newsagent, because in all that time Luc never had a dinnertime unless he went to Michael's. He must have been starving.

Fuck it, said Michael. Fuck the lot of it.

. . . the stony little village and its hedgerow people. This and idiot pigeons, trapped in their indextrous bodies or smushed on roads. The pub's stale carpet, bleached walls, the long, flattening dustfall of its afternoons. Neat houses. Triple glazing. Loft insulation. This and the barbershop's prickly air, its *How's your mum?* as your dad's haircut is imposed on your head. Lost Dog posters. Car seats and kid-leads. Electric gates at the golf course. Your best friend and your wife, fucking. This. And buddleia screaming out from high walls. This and tree roots peeling up pavements like toddlers at wallpaper. The palisade fence around your old school. The rose bush outside the chapel where you first vomited, drunk. Rat shit in the shed. How even this bin holds memories, leaning against it, aged fourteen, waiting for something to happen. This and whitewash in the shoe-shop window. Moths swarming the lamp post. Cats with white snooker-umpire mittens. This and leaves . . .

In a strop once, he kicked his cousin's doll's house in. It felt good – deeply fucking satisfying to stamp a big fuck-off hole through the roof, to crush the smug little chairs and tables, to crumple the floral-wallpapered rooms, to smash the bathtub, the TV, mangling all the little shits who lived inside it, the monstrous little fuckers, sitting round the dinner table, eating their satisfying little meals. Only when he stopped (and he had absolutely no idea why he'd started) and watched her picking up one of the little boys by his remaining arm did he actually realise what he'd done.

She didn't cry, his cousin, who'd been taking the piss out of his outfit. She was fifteen by then, and had only kept the thing because her mum seemed to be attached to the idea of her having a doll's house. She just held up the partially dismembered boy over the house and said,

Wow, Dad was right: you really are a little shit, aren't you?

There was a small face behind the door – Mara, sheepish at the sight of him. He felt so meagre and grateful to see her, still shivering. Crouched, saying *Hello*, with his arms out wide as if to lift her up, to feel the weight of his daughter, her breath at his ear, saying, *Daddy?* in a way that made all of his past feel as though it had a future. To lift her, and feel like a father.

She half-stepped into him – his arms around her – unresponsive.

Get off! Get off! Get off!

He pulled back from the screech, trying to soothe her. She bashed at his arms, punching, as though he was some stranger who'd tried to grab her in the supermarket.

Get off me!

Unleashed, she bounced into the wall, screeched off up the stairs, past Esme's legs – who'd stomped to the door, expecting to have to separate the kids.

Oh, it's you. She's been in one of those moods. Couldn't erase that inheritance, could you?

★

Your moods, she meant. She said it in a way that was designed to sound insincere and uninvolved, but only seemed uninvolved.

Michael didn't tell her about coming across Luc. Or about his walk home. Or all the things he'd raged out of existence. He hadn't kept count.

Where've you been?

Out, he said. Where did you take the kids?

She thought heavily, then

Out.

She drifted off elsewhere. Fogged – barely even speaking to the kids. Bellywoollen's voice could be heard in the inflections through the floorboards, conspiring with Mara. Louis was playing comas on the couch. Michael shut the curtains.

Against the late daylight, he sank into the shed and hid, trying to think of a way out of it all. A route back to work on Monday. To his quiet, stolid life. He started promising himself that it was enough, he'd done enough. He'd find a way, somehow, possibly, of making it up to Julian, of fixing things, somehow. And imagining nothing else. To be innocuous, recessional: he'd done it before, been the kind of man that takes the dog for a walk before work. Whose interaction with the future is to bring a plastic bag with him, in expectation of his dog's tepid shit. Who loves his wife and kids in the things they do, not through what's undone to them. He recovered his life once, didn't he? He could do it again.

*

The wooden slats were furred with cobwebs, and no matter how much he tried to concentrate, every now and then it crept over him. There was too much. It was too various. Even here. And he was responsible for it. He couldn't stop himself. Plant pots (he imagined them). Paint tins (he imagined them). Spiders (he imagined them). The border trimmer they'd used once (he imagined it). All those bags of compost. *That's it*, he told himself, *the last things.*

(Still the thought of Julian's sightless eyes glaring at him and nothing he could do about it. The negation that wouldn't undo a negation.)

Even though he could feel it, thinking of things, an emptiness abscessing, it was almost impossible to comprehend that nothing really existed. Take a boy, imagine him falling from a tree: it's comforting to know that he won't. But there isn't, instead, a nothing boy that falls from a nothing tree. There's his son, who climbed the oak tree at school and sat there, bored – didn't shout at his friends, or throw anything, just sat there till it felt as though he might fall. Which it never did. Because his dad had imagined what that hole might feel like, if he fell through the surface of the world. (Lifting a beer to his mouth, Michael was still shaking, terrified of what he'd done.) It wasn't there before him: there wasn't a Louis-shaped gap in their lives before he was born. Their son had dilated their lives. Cut from them, he'd leave an abyss behind. Because something brings nothing into being. Inscribes a loss. Gives shape and touch to an absence. Can make it breathe and grow. Can, by root or mouth or heart, attach one nothing to another. So, for an almost glimpse in the long blindness of nothing, it can stand in a garden kicking a ball, hold its sister's hand and show her the caterpillars on the leaves, fall asleep in its smallish bed in its smallish house with its parents' heads in the doorway, watching it dream. How something makes our nothings knowable, makes them worthwhile. And though most things don't want to be nothing, everything will.

Here in the shed, in the light of the day's end (he remembered his uncle Mike and June taking him for a walk in the woods with Weldon. The dog vanishing in the ferns, rematerialising on the path in front of them, as though it had travelled thousands of years and back in a few seconds, with nothing to show except a *did you see that?* look on its face, and a green frond in its curls. June asking, *What do you want to be when you grow up?* He probably said *a footballer.* And Uncle Mike sizing him up, *I think you should be a giraffe*) with one bird left on the garden fence, singing hopefully into the grey silence.

After the belated flash of the security light, he caught sight of Esme approaching the shed. She knocked.

All right love, he said.

She hesitated in the doorway, biting her finger. He considered confessing everything – Luc, town, everything. Let the tidal wave of it break over them. He imagined the house washed away. The sight of Esme clinging to a fractured roof beam. Carried away from all this. Before the ocean pulled him under. The thought of Esme being so disappointed in him – *You did this to me.* When there was still a part of him that looked at himself in disbelief, thinking, *But you didn't touch a thing!*

Did you—, she said. Have you—

She groaned and muttered something to herself. Her eyes were red. He dusted the seat with his palm and moved the old computer chair so she could sit down. She didn't.

Is Alex OK? Do you want me to imagine something happening to her?

I don't want you to imagine my sister at all.

She looked at him sternly.

Or Mara. Or Louis. Or me.

He nodded, hesitantly, chastised.

D'you fancy a holiday then?

He knew how ridiculous it sounded. It was all he could bring himself to say.

I mean, we can afford it now. Somewhere nice. Greece? Hawaii?

Esme put her head in her hands, almost smiled.

Have you – what have you imagined about me?

Michael shrugged.

Illnesses, that sort of thing. List stuff. Why?

She looked away, blinking.

What that man said—

Julian, Michael interrupted. He's— that's not what you think. I—

She raised a silencing hand.

You did it, Michael. I know you did. And you can't undo it, can you?

There'll be a way. I'm going to find a way.

She was steady, resigned. Only half in this life.

What he said, about feeling missing. Why do I feel like that?

He shrugged, shaking his head, as if to say *I don't know.*

She made a strange vowel noise. Twisted her lip with a finger and thumb, staring into the dim, lifeless garden, daydreamingly (it was on a train journey, the mountains ignoring them through the window – he'd told her he always wanted to be a sports commentator. She laughed her head on to his shoulder, sweetly, and said, *You can commentate on me if you like? When I go for a jog, or just when I'm at work and stuff.* She swerved when he asked. Said something about needing an *unlived life*. Leaned on him, catching glimpses of the rocks on their slow trek down from thin air) and wound up here, years later, in a shed in a broken place with a man who had no future tense.

Things would happen to them; but nothing they dreamed of.

What've you done to me? There are things I—, she said. I go over things again and again, and there are gaps. I know there are gaps.

Look, what happened with Max—

Max?! Will you stop this – we never had a fucking dog.

What?

(The sound of his bark, the stench of his breath, the heft of him, jumping up on to the sofa and pressing his paws on his chest for a walk, for food, for attention – it was all too real. It all felt so real.)

I'm trying to ask you – I don't know. You just keep going on about this dog you've made up.

Max was. I was walking him—

And inventing all this stuff about us. This mad fantasy life where we went for romantic walks on the beach and had this big wedding – that's not us. It's like we remember completely different lives. What's happening? What have you—

. . .

Michael—

What's going on with you and Luc?

She coughed a laugh, incredulous. Then looked forlorn.

Nothing, she said.

They stared at each other. It was excruciating.

★

If it's what you want to hear, maybe I dreamed of it, yeah. Maybe I dreamed of being with someone who can read a book. Who can cook something other than fish fingers. Maybe I didn't want to be stuck out here, becoming your parents.

Es—

Stuck out here, with kids. Maybe I didn't want kids. Maybe, when I was having a tedious fucking conversation with a three-year-old about a cartoon pig, I dreamed of being elsewhere with, yeah – why not, Luc. Just talking about the news. Or going on holiday to somewhere that didn't have a bastard play area.

Es—

Maybe I fantasised about being with a man who wanted those things too. Someone who I felt connected to. A shared history. And yeah, maybe I thought about fucking him, Michael. Maybe sometimes, I just thought about fucking him. And you know what? Maybe that's what kept me here, with you. The realness of it, the tension of it. That feeling that stops you jumping off the edge of a cliff. That's what's missing. That feels—

Esme—

What?

I—

He had no words.

She stood there coughing. It was dingy in the shed, and she was always prone to a bad chest.

D'you want a drink? I think I've got some ginger ale here somewhere.

You had no right, she coughed.

What have I done?

I don't know. That's what terrifies me.

There was something about the way she held her face that wasn't quite right . . .

I feel trapped – why do I feel trapped? What did you imagine?

What? I—

. . . a slight disresemblance in her expression; her mouth using unfamiliar words, or her eyes not quite used to this light.

Esme?

The way she stood in the shed, blinking, disturbed him.

Why did you marry me? she asked.

Because I love you, he said. Why did you marry me?

She glared at him as though she knew she was supposed to be agitated, or moved, or at least to feel something – as though she was barely here at all. The last few spiders hung awkwardly in the middle of their silence.

Esme?

I'm not sure I can remember.

There was no slamming, no loudness, nothing. Esme drifted from the shed back to the house, gauzily enough to leave the light untroubled.

2

A sleepless night on the sofa. Esme seemed unattached from them, from the idea of them, but he could remind her. He'd piece it all together, he'd bring it to her. Remind her about when they met . . . About moving into the flat above the laundrette with their cheap boxes that fell to pieces, telling the doctor how they got together . . . The trip to A&E, the blood laughing from the tin-can cut on her bare foot . . . All the arguments (hard to think about, even now), shouting over the noise of the road, breaking down each other's defences . . . How they'd extract secrets like fingernails . . . Rotten tooth by rotten tooth, they'd root out the worst of each other, and hold it in their palm as if it was nothing . . . All that mess, so that when they were alone with each other under the soft light of the television, they wore a face that only the other had seen. It took so much effort to be that ugly for each other. So much love. If she'd kept them alive in her mind all through the coma, it was his turn now.

Hazily, he decided to go for a walk to get the words straight in his head, how he'd clarify, explain, begin to repair their life. *Esme, I know . . .* or *Esme, we can . . .* Hopefully something would come next. So in a daze of the past, he stepped out to one of those hyper-blue days, where the sky is thinly painted and bleaches towards the ground. One of those days where you're halfway up the street before you notice the cars, the houses, trees. Or the gaps where they used to be.

Shit.

Half of the estate was missing.

Michael turned to dart back to the house, but the woman from two doors down had spotted him in her periphery, staring at the sky as though she had a vision from some dream where she'd lived eight feet up in the empty air. He swerved again – made his way, hurriedly, anywhere.

At the edge of the estate, the street sign was blank.

He found himself drawn to the holloway. There was no holloway, no wood. Lining the edge of its path-lopped roots, nothing much. A few unlikely trees, limping on broken-branch crutches.

There were no leaves. There was no grass. The snail shells were empty by the kerbs.

The golf course fence, gone. The substation, gone. Nobody was playing on the mud. Only a gang of dogs, hunting gulls into the bunkers.

Everything seemed startled.

*

Why did he walk here? The whole town was broken into glances. Catching himself suspiciously in the corner of his eye. There on the windows of the charity shop. The laundrette. The parked cars.

The post office was missing. The chemist.

Half-sketched trees reached out into the whiteness.

People were going about their business unreally, as if they were in the opening credits to a kids' TV show. Or else grazing this nowhere, dazed.

Even though he believed he had done it, Michael couldn't believe he had done it.

Here was the delirious, birdbrained vision of the town. Here was the rage back home.

You could see right through a hole in the oak to the estate, as though it had grown around a necessary absence. He into it.

If they moved back here – if he'd brought Esme back here – because it was comfortable, because he was already here, waiting, his name scratched into the bus stop that was now hollow air, fattened in the chippy that was an empty scrut of stony ground between the dry cleaner and the charity shop, staring into the pond that was a splotch of drying mud, then what? The place had abbreviated. Crows hung about on the green, on the benches, cawing apostrophes. Everyone looked as though they'd forgotten what they'd come out for: daffodils in midwinter spring, lolling, confused, in the blankness.

Excuse me, mate. You couldn't point me the way to the train station?

A familiar voice.

Excuse me—

Michael couldn't pretend not to have heard him. When he turned, there was no recognition on Luc's face. He looked as though he'd slept rough and was about to ask another stranger for a few coins to help him on his way home.

For an awkward moment they stared at one another. Then,

Excuse me, said Luc. I've gone on holiday by mistake, are you the farmer?

This giggle frothed from him irrepressibly, a shaken, half-cracked beer can of a giggle. It unnerved Michael. Luc coming back here with less and less of himself intact. Back here for his childhood. Or back here for Esme. If he'd even gone home last night. (At thirteen, they pushed Luc's dad's TV off the edge of the abandoned quarry – a big, boxy TV with a dead body's weight. Michael gave the final heft. The reckless gravity of it, that piece of Luc's dad's house crashing down the bank, coming apart because he'd pushed it, made him swear to himself not to go near the edge of anything again. But Luc laughed.) And he wasn't even sure Luc recognised him. But that kind of cascading laughter. It was hard not to be drawn into his energy, as though the whole thing was an elaborate joke.

Sorry, he tried to contain himself. Sorry.

Then collapsed in hysterics. Now Michael, too, felt shaken loose of everything, laughing: the gaps, the nothings, his family – it was ridiculous. His friend was a mess: his suit was covered in dirt and there was what looked like bird crap on his lapel, but that was probably something he'd mostly eaten. But here they were like teenagers again, in Jack Baillie's caravan, stoned or half- or mostly drunk, laughing at the things that always made them laugh.

Luc gathered himself.

I'm sorry. You couldn't point me in the direction of the train station, could you?

And the laughter calcified on Michael's face.

It's been a while since I've lived here. Things seem to have changed.

This man had no idea who he was. A little cough, a hesitation – and out of a sense of not wanting to cause a fuss, Michael nodded and pointed ahead, kindly helping a stranger.

Yeah, if you follow that road you'll see a sign for it. It's not far.

Thank you. Thanks very much. Thanks.

(All of his life: *Don't cause a fuss.* As if there was one rule. His mum tugging his whiny arm in the supermarket, *Don't cause a fuss.*)

No problem.

Luc started with a little backstep, as though he needed a run-up, but then examined Michael.

Hang on, he said.

Shit, Michael? Fucking hell mate, how are things?

Michael shrugged, off-beat.

Fuck – it's been—

Luc was rubbing his forehead for words.

Yeah, said Michael. Hi,—

Shitting hell. You look great.

Well, Michael forced a smile. You too.

Luc cackled.

Hey, at our age you get the face you deserve.

They both tried to find it funny. Neither quite did.

So how are things. Didn't you marry, er, what's her?

Esme? Yeah. Two kids.

Fucking hell, said Luc, shaking his hand, as though Esme was the last name he expected him to say. Congratulations, mate, congratulations.

And you?

He felt compelled to ask, terrified of an answer. Lucas looked confused, struggling to remember what he'd been doing for days, weeks, months at a time.

He snapped out of his daze.

We should go for a drink! Not now, I have to get back to—. I've got to get back. But we'll go for a drink. Let's go for a drink.

Michael nodded.

Fuck. We were—

Luc measured their boyhood height with his hand, started chuckling as though he'd remembered something.

Wow, mate. Look, I've got to go. But it's good to see you – you look great.

Yeah, you too.

Give my love to the family, he said over his shoulder. Walked away, clapped in amazement.

*

Dizzily, Michael eased himself on to a nearby bench. He felt as though he was going to black out. Head sunk between his legs; a cold sweat. The voice in his head trying to find words that weren't *what the fuck?*

He remembered Luc screaming at his dad's front door, *I never asked to be born.* And the voice of his dad from inside: *You think you're special? No fucker did.* Walking back to Michael's, where Luc lived for the next few months. The pair of them with food poisoning from the dodgy chippy that same night; cramped into Michael's room, buckets at their bedsides, feeling as though their whole life was being stripped from them, retch by retch, and then at daft-in-the-morning, when they caught each other's eye, vomiting, and began giggling. Giggling and vomiting, vomiting and laughing, vomiting hysterics. When they finally coughed to a halt, bile in the back of their noses, and Luc said, *Shame we didn't die then. Would've been a good story, that.*

All the way home he thought of how he was going to convince Esme that they needed to leave urgently without frightening her. One look out of the window and she'd see the damage. He didn't want her to become one of his absences, to leave him, saying she *couldn't risk the kids*, couldn't risk herself. The further she broke from him, the nearer she was to the cliff edge of his imagination. The anxiety that there's no totally safe way to be a woman in the mind of a man.

He could see all the way over to the lump, bare of its old church and its gravestones where he wittered on at Esme about something he knew, or half-knew, about the tidemarks of invasions on the chapel walls – when it had only been a month, maybe two months, and she'd insisted on coming out to meet his parents, and somehow there he was talking about bomb damage to a roof on a chapel that neither of them gave a shit about when she stopped him with a punch on the arm and said, *Do you love me yet?*

Two months. Maybe it was three, or four. She was smiling, but not as though it was a joke. He stood there, saying, *Er, er, er, er.*

Of course he loved her. How could he not love her with a question like that?

Their house fell up bold as a show house, expecting the others to arrive from that brown mess around it any minute.

She hadn't heard him come in, standing in the kitchen in her pyjamas with her back to the door, chopping strawberries and singing along to the radio. Seeing her like that solved everything; they didn't have to be afraid. These walls, the houses, the town – he could erase the lot if it meant that they could begin again. Nothing mattered. And – from time to time he had these cute moments of ingenuity – that's it: he'd go (and everything would be well again, no more strange looks or awkward touches, no more hesitations, no more almost utterances), he'd go and with a light punch on the arm he'd ask her, *Do you love me, yet?*

The cut smell of strawberries, syruping the air. He could barely hold back the smile as he approached on his lightest footsteps. She hadn't seen him, hadn't felt him. Until, with the lightest of punches, she screamed.

Who the fuck are you?

She pointed the knife at him.

I— I—.

What are you doing here? Just—

Michael was holding his hands out.

Esme, it's OK.

What the fuck? How do you know my name? Who are you?

She squinted at him, as though she was trying to place a voice far off, saying *Uhs-me.*

Esme, he pleaded. It's me.

Get out!

She sounded unsure of herself.

Get the fuck out!

She felt for her phone without taking her eyes off him. She had Esme's face, but not in the way Esme would wear it.

I'm phoning the police, she said.

Kids ran in from the garden; she shouted at them to stay away, keeping the kitchen knife pointed at Michael. They tilted their heads, owlish, eyeing this almost unplaceable man, who'd maybe stepped out from the TV, or had been left behind by a dream.

What the fuck are you doing in my house?

She jarred at *my house.* The apparition of this man in the kitchen seemed to make her second-guess why she was out here, slicing strawberries in a discreet house on the outskirts, as though she'd woken up in the middle of somebody else's life.

Esme—

Get out!

Esme – I'm your husband.

He didn't know who he was trying to convince.

She was crying, confused and terrified, pointing the knife. He backed away.

We had a life together.

It sounded pointless.

Even now, as he was retreating towards the door, he was imagining himself being stabbed by a woman who was nobody. Or not nobody. A woman surprised to find she was pointing a knife at a man in her house. A woman who looked worried she was losing it.

You don't remember me, he said. But I love you.

Hearing himself, he realised how ridiculous it was.

She paused for a moment (he remembered Esme coming to at the dentist, wisdom-toothless and in a strange room), a held hand to the side of her face.

Get out! You fucking weirdo – get out!

I—. Esme, I didn't mean for this to happen. I love you.

Out!

He backed out of the door. She locked it behind him.

Her face appeared in the living-room window, drawing the curtains. Almost closed, she hesitated, staring at him.

Maybe, he hoped, she might still recognise something in him. It could all be undone, remade. If she could just find the faintest resemblance, staring at this man on the bald grass outside the house, staring back.

The curtain closed.

He crouched, holding his chest in the breathless air.

There was the sound of blood in his ear.

Through the thin cloud, the light held his shadow aside from him, one hand touching the side of their head.

Stupefied, trying to make sense of things: Michael at his parents' door. He found he'd let himself in. Sat himself down.

He could hear his parents in other rooms. This room was quiet with photographs. Across the tables and the walls, on the mantelpiece and windowsill, placed in any old frame (him as a baby – some holiday to a damp beach – him on Uncle Mike's shoulders – one of his dad as a kid, standing on the wrecked house, the man in the background holding a broom, not knowing where to begin). He couldn't remember any of them being taken. These lives in parenthesis, warding off forgetting.

From the kitchen, his mum's voice, talking on the phone. He felt twelve years old, waiting for her to finish the call with his headteacher. *OK . . . OK . . . Bye then. Bye.* The sound of the fridge-freezer door. Glass, ice cubes. Her unmistakable footsteps.

★

(All of his small years, tucked in bed, listening for those footsteps below, willing her to come upstairs and talk him to sleep.)

Approaching. He didn't dare look at the doorway.

No, no—

She spilled her drink when she walked in the room – wavered a vowel. Crouched to wet carpet automatically, gaping at him.

Reached out – not daring to touch, half to hold him off.

His dad came shuffling after –

Suze?

presuming she'd tripped.

Their slack, question-mark mouths punctuated the wordlessness. Afraid to ask how he'd come home and was sitting there, so usual, so changed.

Michael?

His doubtful name was a nudge for explanation. He half-smiled, uselessly.

Are you here? Please don't lie to me, Michael. Please.

I—

He let the words fade from his face. They were clinging on him, some hesitant miracle. He couldn't stop it, the memory of them approaching the marvel of his hospital bed, not quite allowing themselves to believe that their son wouldn't slip back from them. (He dug his thumbs into his eyes to blot it out.) Whatever they thought had happened to him, whatever story they'd told themselves, was having to be readjusted, urgently, tentatively – their lost boy who rematerialised one day in the living room.

I'm sorry, he said. This was a mistake.

They jolted as he stood. His dad held a pleading hand out for him to stay. They looked as though they were dealing with a bear.

It's OK, his dad calmed. You're OK.

Michael was pressing his face. His mind repeating *What are you doing here? What are you doing here?* Retreating home. He'd destroyed his family. So here he was, looking to belong to something. Somewhere to be familiar. Somewhere to apply the pressure of his being alive that would keep his shape. The groove he thought he had worn in his parents. Who were gawping at him: this inexplicable thing.

You won't understand. But I've done something terrible.

No, said his dad. No – don't be daft, son, you wouldn't do anything that bad.

He smiled awkwardly.

His mum caught him looking at the photos of him as a boy, as though this man was trying to recognise himself. The house was sleepy with them. And his sleepy parents, trying to wake themselves from a strange dream where their little boy walked into the house in a man's body.

Are you OK, son?

His dad seemed more certain of him. Or more willing to entertain the idea that this was his boy.

I didn't realise, said Michael. All this time, I didn't realise what I was doing.

It's OK, son. You can tell us.

After the coma—

His mum and dad glanced at each other, as though this was new information.

When I got home, I could barely remember anything. And it was so disorientating and—

(He could see himself sitting in this chair, crying. He closed his eyes, coughed – tried to clear his mind.)

I can imagine things out of existence. Like that cup – I could imagine it, and it'd disappear. Or I could imagine you tripping over, and you wouldn't.

His mum gripped his dad's arm. They were crying.

But – I didn't know. Everything I remembered – being with Esme, with the kids. I thought I was getting them back. I thought I was bringing it all back, but it's gone. Everything I remembered – it's like it never happened. I've undone it.

They were confused –

She doesn't know who I am. She can't remember me.

strained their eyes at him, as though they were trying to make out a face, approaching far off.

Mum?

He could see himself. (He thought about stopping it. He didn't stop it.) He could see himself sitting on this chair, his school uniform torn – a scrap with one of the posh kids, or something – and that teenage fury of individuation, thinking *they don't get it*, refusing responsibility. Ridding himself of himself, he let it all pour back: the banalities of being a family, of TV together, of eating together, of letting time accrue in each other's company, the shape of this room containing his idea of home, the angle of its lightfall, the colour of his days. He remembered being there, in front of the fireplace, his mum crouched down on the carpet beside him, cheering and smiling when he found the right piece of the puzzle and locked it into place. His mum lying down there, singing, his head on her chest, listening to her voice fill the empty spaces inside her.

His mum grabbed his dad's arm.

Frank, it's not him. Why isn't it him?

She turned to Michael, her face in despair –

Why are you doing this to us? Why are you pretending to be my son? What's the matter with you?

Michael edged past them, keeping their nervous distance. His dad was holding his mum, crying into his shoulder.

I'd better go, said Michael.

As though he was late to pick the kids up from their gymnastics class. As though he had somewhere else to be.

He turned back to face his childhood. This house – its white walls and wide eyes, the rose bush that woke up yearly by the front window, the certainty of the low wall outside where he practised shots into the bottom corner: whatever else happened, whatever tide approached, somehow it was here, holding his childhood together against everything falling to pieces. It was the kind of future he thought Esme wanted for their family. The kind of future he wanted. And if he took one step further back, it felt like he'd fall off the edge of a cliff.

Michael stood where the accident happened, staring at the grassless earth. He thought of Max, sitting there like that sad dog from the painting. Bent down to the bare ground, as the world might regrow around him. Thinking, *If I could remember the golf ball hitting my head—*

I

He was still on the ground when the emergency services arrived with a careful hand on his shoulder. They said something things. Watery-sounding; his ears submerged.

He'd been motioned into the back of the ambulance. The siren wasn't sounding. *At least I'm not an emergency*, he thought. But the straps were reassuring, because everything else felt light and unattached. He imagined the ambulance hitting a kerb and toppling – and him, suspended in mid-air, bound in this seat, Esme standing horizontally where the back door was bust open, shaking her head at him.

Last time this happened, he said, I had a dog.

There was a touch on his arm. A sympathetic look.

No, it's my fault. So vivid, when I woke from my coma. I vanished him with my thoughts.

The paramedic had a practised neutral face.

That's not the least of it, he laughed. You should ask my wife.

The ambulance shunted over a speedbump. Michael was smiling to himself, delirious.

D'you think you can fix that?

Something was needled into his arm. Some numbness, unravelling through his veins.

His dad (for a moment he panicked about his dad) half-dipped the fish he'd caught that time in the cold river, in the other hand his knife, and unseamed it along the belly to let its fluids unspool along the current, till the shape of the fish stared dumbly at nothing and the water flowing through it ran clear.

It had gone. Everything he remembered had gone.

Michael felt the door close on him, that dusk feeling in his bloodstream, filling his limbs, his torso, all the way up to his neck, the back of his skull; just the pale square of the hospital window to give the world a shape.

They'd left him in a hospital bed in an empty room. If anyone had been to investigate him, he hadn't been awake. Or if not, then they had come through the room as sideways as a dream. It didn't really matter where he was, now. He didn't feel as though he was anywhere.

Daydreaming – picturing a villa where they swam in the morning and in the afternoon ate barbequed prawns with their feet dipped in the sea. Or up on fire-watch in some mountain shack, where the kids learned all about the life cycles of the forest and they washed their faces in their own reflections in the glacial lake.

Or in cities. Mansions. On farms. Beach huts. All of the lives they promised themselves late at night, the futures that fell through afternoons, the worlds they dreamed of waking to.

He'd spent so long trying not to think of anything good in their future that it felt intoxicating, reckless, imagining himself walking across the meadow back to their cottage, where Esme was outside drinking pomegranate juice, the warm sun so low he only had to raise his arm for his shadow to reach her.

Nobody came. There was only the pale-blue room, the electric light and the shadow-flit of some insect for company.

Every future that appealed to him, he'd erased. Cancelled lives, compressing him into this small room.

Everything he remembered, excavated. Hollowing himself.

He lay on the hospital bed, thinking Esme would be furious with him. Saying *What the hell have you done now?*

Remembering himself out of existence.

Michael slipped beneath the skin of his eyelids. Hid there. With his wife. With his children.

O

There were days and days, and most days were a way of forgetting. The showers, the breakfasts, the school runs . . . Gone, except in accretion. The days that thicken on us.

But memory was relief, dissolution – a vanishing act from the light of one place into the light of another. Remembering packing sandwiches in the slightly disconcerting smell that wouldn't wash from Louis' lunchbox. The paler carpet around the furniture. Toothpaste dribbles sputtered and cleaned away in the same places on the bathroom floor. The splits in the binding of *The Tiger Who Came to Tea* and how Mara would crawl over him and growl when he called her his *little tiger cub*. The aches in the spine of the stairs. The dockyard holler of their house on a morning. (Outside the bedroom window: the nervous branch, the sound of a small leaf testing its voice.)

Dinnertimes, bathtimes, bedtimes. He remembered the way small people blast a lifetime from a minute. How only Esme was allowed to brush Louis' hair. Only Michael was allowed to tie Mara's shoes. How bad the kids were at hiding things: behind the curtains, underneath their beds, inside their shoes. Until they stopped using the house's dark places and kept things beneath their skins instead. (A little girl trips on the stairs up to her brother's bedroom, waking him up, *Do you want to play?*) He remembered the exhaustion: arguing with it, negotiating with it, trying to forget it was happening to him. And Esme saying, in what sounded like a foreign language, *You're tired?*

Trips to the doctor. Trips to the dentist. Nursing fevers, chickenpox, hand, foot and mouth. Spoonfuls and spoonfuls of Calpol. The ingot of a poorly kid in a crib. The feel of the back of his hand on her forehead, on his forehead. The way the children's sicknesses multiplied in them. (From the dull forest loam one pushes, hopefully – now another.) Esme standing outside the door to Louis' room, prodding Michael's anxious chest, *He's a boy, not a vase – they mend when they break.* The way she could put a child to bed as though she was planting a landmine. (Soon the whole floor is febrile: a rash of bluebells, blazing all through the wood.)

First steps in the garden. Spring's midsummer weekends. The kids inventing games that never began, their reality nudging his aside. The feeling that growing older is the slow insanity of believing too much in yourself. As he remembered being in gardens and games (She has this dream: a man, her husband, is in a hospital bed and she's given up hope. This moth, this infuriating moth – so meagre, with so much more life than him – has landed on his forehead; she smashes it, there, with a magazine. He wakes up! She wakes up.) and that feeling at the end of a busy day, when he'd close his eyes with the children's voices still playing in his head.

He remembered teaching her how to iron, now that they were responsible adults and could no longer afford creases. Coming home to the flat, swaddling tarka dhal and rice, coming home with stories of passive aggression at the printer, realpolitik in the staff kitchen, restructuring, bogus claims procedures, Fiona's soup-labelling – he remembered how she pretended to listen, kissed him on the cheek when he was done. (The cleaners have finished vacuuming the office, chattering as they run cloths over the desks, sunlight catching the motes where they rise.)

He remembered hiding up trees. Behind bushes and doors. In cubicles and cloakrooms. From phone calls and emails and doorbells. In cars. Behind bins and geography classrooms. Under railway bridges. Once in a culvert. (He's at his desk before he takes off his sunglasses – the light is overwhelming, as though he'd just stepped out, midsummer, from a cave. His pupils soon narrow sense from things.) Hiding in Esme's cupboard in her flat – how had he got in? – waiting to jump out on her. But she came in on the phone, talking about him: nothing special, just that he was coming round later and *yeah, it's going really well – he's really sweet.* He'd never felt so absent: jumping out of the cupboard now would have been as though he'd jumped out on himself. As though her subconscious had materialised him. He waited between her dresses until she went to the bathroom, snuck out through her window hoping that nobody called the police.

Camille. Kirsty. Jenny. Siobhan. How he could fall in love from the way they laughed or ignored him or, with their hair up, just from the backs of their necks. How the heart has room for lifetimes of love, but our lives are small and can only carry so much. (Bees tremble, fuzzy and vicarious; in the verges, on the roundabouts, through the bed outside the pub, from the window ledge of the chemist – all through the town the flowers are fucking one another. The county judges are impressed.) They all seemed so much better at the world than he did, all had so much more about them. He remembered wanting to learn how he moved through all those beautiful heads.

He remembered piss-ups and hangovers. Deadlines and hangovers. The grease in their student house that seemed to move independently, the mould on their walls with its own intelligence. The way the years passed by in parenthesis, with people he can barely recall, in moods that felt as though they belonged in a different body. (The sun comes out in a beer garden; they're scouring social media, trying to remember whatshisface's name, and face. He puts his phone down a second to take off his jacket. A small bird lands by their table, hops, twitches, flits away.) Queueing to change his course. Sitting on his coat on the grass with a book he didn't understand about a prison, feeling the spring warmth through the thatched shadow of the tree, as if this was supposed to be university, the pigeons in the periphery, watching him.

Playing football half-cut at night, floodlit in the car park by the old air-raid shelter. (The season opens with an empty seat beside him, folded. But as the results pick up, it's taken by a bloke who likes lukewarm Dr Pepper Zero, believes wholeheartedly in two up top and eats pies with his mouth open. An eighty-fifth-minute own goal, the bloke clatters down in the seat and he loses it, pointing at his pie-smeared face, *My son's seat! You're sitting in my son's seat!* Remembers himself – not making any sense – leaves, for the first time, before the final whistle. Buys a ticket for a different stand.) Remembered Jonno with a wild clearance and himself volleying it clean through the gap in the fence, shattering the night where it lay on number forty-two's front window. The feeling of disappearing like hares into nowhere.

Shouting *Shit!* when it was too late, Luc glaring at him as though he'd really gone and done it now. Remembered the whole class gasping at the sight of Lia standing in the shock of being completely drenched in hydrochloric acid. All the faff of tragedy petered out when it transpired, five minutes later, there'd only be a tiny splash on her jumper. (The police tape off the road. There isn't much left for people to see – the odd bit of smashed-in tail light, waiting to be picked up. The flowers beginning to bloom along the roadside fence.) But no one said anything as Michael expected them to, like *Fucking spaz hands! OH MY GOD you've burnt all her skin off! I swear down, if she hadn't been wearing safety goggles, they'd be measuring her up for a guide dog now. ARE YOU GONNA PAY FOR HER PLASTIC SURGERY THEN, OR WHAT? Dickhead*. Everyone gathering around Lia, leaving him; his guilt untouched, standing by the desk holding a scratched penny, as though he'd never happened.

Lessons and lessons and lessons. Life crammed in between. And because Jenny was playing in it, he auditioned for the school production of *Cardenio* where he scored a role as the tree. In one scene she crept on all fours under Michael's legs and crouched there with her mouth and eyes near his groin. (She keeps brushing her hair behind her ears and letting it fall when she laughs; between courses, he says *You've got a beautiful mouth.*) The leaves they'd glued to him plucked off little bits of skin. In the shower, the last few blotched and mulched from him down the drain.

Breaking into barns. Drinking behind the church hall. Walking along the railway line – September, their football shirts were still far too big for them, getting snagged on the brambles. Luc insisted him along. *A bit further. A bit further.* (From the lofty office window, he could see across the city's haze, packed in by the vague greenness that was his childhood, the loneliness of woods. The lift's downward rush elates him back to the business of the street. He looks at himself in the plate-glass windows. He's smiling, meeting her for lunch.) He was terrified a train would come. Or somebody would see them. Or he'd step on a live line somewhere and be blasted into the future. But Luc was right – even though it took them far longer to get there. She was topless, sunbathing in her back garden. Luc already digging around the bottom of the siding after some gas canister he reckoned was down there – as if he'd brought Michael because Michael needed to see. He looked, he definitely looked. But after a minute or so he still hadn't really worked out how he was supposed to be looking. *What if a train comes?*

Wedding flowers. Birthday flowers. The flowers at his granddad's funeral said 'Dad', which was when it properly struck him that Dad had a dad, and that was Granddad. The war people called him 'Spud' (the first Michael had heard of it): the best mate anyone could hope for in a POW camp. (The green bolt of a damselfly shoots across the black surface of the pond and off between the market stalls, where the greengrocer calls the price of strawberries like some prophet. It takes to people's heads.) Wanting to cry, but his dad was, and that was too weird. Uncle Cal stepping out, wiping the sweat from his eyes and whistling the theme tune to *Dad's Army*. Michael was disappointed they'd burnt him, now that he was grown up enough to throw a bit of earth on the coffin. Staring at the floor. All the shadows of the adults talking about things that happened before he was born.

The paler daylight through their bedroom curtains, and his dad shuttling out through the door. *Why don't you do something nice for your mum and tidy your room?* He was good at tidying his room; so much would fit under his bed. The smallest piece of a Russian doll that he'd stolen from Nanny's collection. The littlest one was the realest one and all the others were pretending. He remembered that because Mum was poorly, he dusted and sprayed and tidied everything up *spick and span*. (From under the shed, the slugs emerge. Next door's cat alerts the garden light. The slugs' histories glister across the grass.) When he saw her grappling to the bathroom with a hand on the side of her face, he called and tugged at her to look. Her free hand brushed his head as she passed, as though he was a leaf.

Uncle Mike has gone to live as an American, his mum answered. He remembered her saying that one morning as he was eating his Corn Flakes and thinking that Uncle Mike would be like one of those actors in a cereal advert, whose mouth moved the American way but sounded different. *Why?* he asked, and she dropped her marmalade-heavy toast. The kitchen floor always had to be clean. She screamed and screamed when he walked through in his football boots. Even Weldon knew not to visit with sticky paws. Michael thought his mum would've liked it in America. On the TV, everything looked clean. He imagined living in a skyscraper, with the clouds pouring down his windows, but probably not for long. (The kids were hard to keep up with in the park; she stopped for a moment to catch her breath – watched the geese, restive on the water, threatening to lift their reflections from underneath the lake. *Wait up!* she shouted to the girl.)

Uncle Mike lifting him out of a strop and carrying him on his shoulders through the fields, pointing out all the places where he used to build dens, the barns that were haunted, all the good spots for setting ambushes. He remembered feeling as giant as the pylons, making enormous strides across the earth. *You wanna build a T-rex trap?* He dug a hole with his hands. *What's a hole made of?* They ripped off young branches to cover it, baited it with crisps. (She pulls over to let the ambulance by, trundling up the road like an urgent wardrobe.) His uncle recalling Michael about all of the other things he'd caught – a leopard, an alien, June – and how you could tell there were dinosaurs between here and the motorway from the patterns the ants made harvesting his Rice Krispies. How it was dark on the way home and they had to be quiet – *Listen – can you hear it?* – because the pylons were humming the prelude from *Tristan und Isolde.* Which was why his mum's voice sounded so loud when they got to the front door and she shouted, *Michael!*

His job to check all of the plants in the allotment for holes in the leaves – but he remembered liking *The Very Hungry Caterpillar.* Liking it so much he ripped the pages out and kept them with him and his mum screamed, *No! Michael!* (She crouches as low as she can, scooping a hole in the flower bed and hoping that it's not too early, that there won't be another frost, the weather being so hard to judge now; she loved them, those big, smiling heads of the sunflowers – they grow up so quickly.) Mum reading 'Jack and Jill': it made him sadder than he could understand. Throwing coins down the wishing well. His seemed to take forever, and when he looked up his mum wasn't smiling.

He remembered bathtime: his mum warming his pyjamas on the radiator for when he got out. His superhero figures fighting underwater. Spinning the bath up with a finger until a whirlpool formed, throwing in the men to their deaths. The blizzards of talcum powder. (Kids are playing outside their house in the snow – underneath the bare branches, their voices in the thin winter air, the closeness of departed things. And she thinks how old he would be now, if everything – and sits in the rich, snowlight of the room, rubbing her hand back and forth across, comfortingly, slowly back and forth.) He remembered his mum lifting him from the bath and wrapping him in the warm towel while he screamed and screamed as though he'd been lifted out of the world – how he wished she'd go away forever and leave him alone.

Rain on the cover of his buggy, the world blurred grey. The blurred, block colours of his parents – red coat, green coat – moving around him, as though he was somewhere else completely (through the cloudy window at the city, where it leans from the underground, she fantasises again of a quiet life: sensible husband, kids, suburbs, dogs – one of those painless lives, free from worry, from fear – feeling, almost, as though it was worn in, there, waiting for her, if she just stayed on the train . . . But always, she alighted at the next station, her mind back on work, on the work she'd promised, with the voices of the engines and the deaf birds and unstoppable city surging right) looking back at them.

–1

Although it's late now, you see the dark square of the hospital window move into the pale; it never stops – porters taking white sheets to the morgue, blue lights flashing by the entrance. That anything arrives is incidental; nothing so easily departs. There is fear in the water fountains, in the wrist tags, in the curtains. Fear shouts from the lintels, in the gutters. Fear lies softly in the grass by the car park, where a mind is struggling to make sense of the parking meter, and now is also footfalls marking the corridors and sickly wheels on polished floors. The automatic coughs of workmen, mending walls. This is one of those places that will outlive itself, the way the graveyard seems more alive than the church. Outside, last year's leaves survive in the reach of the bare branch tapping the window. Sometimes it feels like a lowered voice behind a curtain. Sometimes it feels like a crash-call alarm. While they're fastening tags to tiny wrists, anxieties, by the vending machine, wait. A woman smokes by the quiet doors, chewing her thumb. Our undoing won't leave us undone. But for however long, you hold it together. And in the room you are thinking of, where the orderly has stripped the empty bed and is tucking clean sheets, and stops for a second, confused by the shadow – from the chair? from the door? – that looked for all the world like the shadow of a person shielding their eyes, as though they were following the flight of something struck into the distance on a sunlit day.

Acknowledgements

Thank you, Matthew Marland at RCW.

Thank you, Lettice Franklin at W&N.

Thank you, New Writing North.

Thank you, Peter Mawdsley.

Thank you, Deryn Rees-Jones.

Thank you, Gill, Sarah, Elwood and Elijah.

Thank you, Mick, Andrea, Bobby and Ted.

Thank you, Matty.

Thank you, Mam and Dad.

Thank you, thank you, thank you, Em.

About the Author

Daniel O'Connor is a lecturer in English Literature and Creative Writing at the University of Liverpool and author of *Ted Hughes and Trauma: Burning the Foxes*, published by Palgrave Macmillan. Previously, he worked as a bookseller in London and Liverpool. He was born in Middlesbrough and lives in North Wales.

Help us make the next generation of readers

We – both author and publisher – hope you enjoyed this book. We believe that you can become a reader at any time in your life, but we'd love your help to give the next generation a head start.

Did you know that 9 per cent of children don't have a book of their own in their home, rising to 13 per cent in disadvantaged families*? We'd like to try to change that by asking you to consider the role you could play in helping to build readers of the future.

We'd love you to think of sharing, borrowing, reading, buying or talking about a book with a child in your life and spreading the love of reading. We want to make sure the next generation continue to have access to books, wherever they come from.

And if you would like to consider donating to charities that help fund literacy projects, find out more at **www.literacytrust.org.uk** and **www.booktrust.org.uk**.

THANK YOU

*As reported by the National Literacy Trust